"I didn't think you wanted to get involved. What changed your mind?"

His gaze was riveted to hers. Intense. Compelling. "You."

There was so much feeling behind that one word. She attempted a laugh that came out shaky.

"So you're taking Shep?"

"Maybe. If we're a good fit. I've been reading up on service dogs."

She shooed him outside. "Then go see Shep."

His chuckles lingered in the air as he left. The sound warmed her. She closed her eyes for a moment, immediately picturing the laugh lines at the corners of his eyes deepening and the edges of his mouth tilting up. The image sent goose bumps spreading over her. She rubbed her hands up and down her arms as though she could erase his effect on her.

Books by Margaret Daley

Love Inspired

*Gold in the Fire
*A Mother for Cindy
*Light in the Storm
 The Cinderella Plan
*When Dreams Come True
 Hearts on the Line
*Tidings of Joy
 Heart of the Amazon
†Once Upon a Family
†Heart of the Family
†Family Ever After
 A Texas Thanksgiving
†Second Chance Family
†Together for the Holidays
††Love Lessons
††Heart of a Cowboy
††A Daughter for Christmas
**His Holiday Family
.**A Love Rekindled
**A Mom's New Start
§§Healing Hearts
§§Her Holiday Hero

Love Inspired Suspense

So Dark the Night
Vanished

Buried Secrets
Don't Look Back
Forsaken Canyon
What Sarah Saw
Poisoned Secrets
Cowboy Protector
Christmas Peril
 "Merry Mayhem"
§Christmas Bodyguard
Trail of Lies
§Protecting Her Own
§Hidden in the Everglades
§Christmas Stalking
Detection Mission
§Guarding the Witness

*The Ladies of
 Sweetwater Lake
†Fostered by Love
††Helping Hands
 Homeschooling
**A Town Called Hope
§Guardians, Inc.
§§Caring Canines

MARGARET DALEY

feels she has been blessed. She has been married more than thirty years to her husband, Mike, whom she met in college. He is a terrific support and her best friend. They have one son, Shaun. Margaret has been writing for many years and loves to tell a story. When she was a little girl, she would play with her dolls and make up stories about their lives. Now she writes these stories down. She especially enjoys weaving stories about families and how faith in God can sustain a person when things get tough. When she isn't writing, she is fortunate to be a teacher for students with special needs. Margaret has taught for more than twenty years and loves working with her students. She has also been a Special Olympics coach and has participated in many sports with her students.

Her Holiday Hero
Margaret Daley

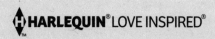

Recycling programs
for this product may
not exist in your area.

™ LOVE INSPIRED BOOKS

ISBN-13: 978-0-373-81735-1

HER HOLIDAY HERO

www.Harlequin.com

Printed in U.S.A.

God is our refuge and strength,
a very present help in trouble.
—*Psalms* 46:1

Chapter One

Jake Tanner had pulled out the desk chair in his home office and started to sit when the front doorbell chimed in the blissful quiet. He would never take silence for granted again. A long breath swooshed from his lungs as he straightened and gripped his cane, then limped toward the foyer. Through the long, narrow window with beveled glass, he could make out his neighbor standing on the porch.

Marcella Kime found a reason to see him at least a couple of times a week. He'd become her mission since he'd returned home to Cimarron City from serving in the military overseas. A few days earlier she'd jokingly told him she missed her grandson, and he would do just fine taking his place. He still wasn't sure what to make of that statement. He had returned to Cimarron City, a town he'd lived in for a while and visited often to see his grandma. Dealing with family, especially his father, the general, had been too much for him three months ago when he'd been released from the military hospital.

He swung the door open to reveal Marcella, probably no more than five feet tall, if that, with her hands full. "Good morning." She smiled as she juggled a large box and a plate of pastries. He reached for the parcel.

"The Fed Ex guy left this late yesterday afternoon. I meant to bring it over sooner, but then I had to go to church to help with the pancake supper. You're always home so I was surprised he couldn't deliver the package."

"Went to the VA hospital in Oklahoma City."

"Oh, good. You went out." She presented the plate of goodies. "I baked extra ones this morning because I know how much you enjoy my cinnamon rolls. I'm going to put those pounds you lost back on in no time. I imagine all those K rations aren't too tasty."

"I haven't had MREs—meals ready to eat—in six months, and no, they aren't tasty. In the hospital I was fed regular meals." But he hadn't wanted to eat much. He was working out again and building up his muscles at least.

"Oh, my. *K rations* certainly dates me. That's what they were called when my older brother was in the army."

His seventy-five-year-old neighbor with stark white hair never was at a loss for words. After she left, his head would throb from all the words tumbling around inside. He wanted to tell her again that she didn't need to worry about him, that in time his full appetite would return, but she continued before he could open his mouth.

"I'd come in, but I have to leave. Saturday is my day to get my hair washed and fixed. It needs it. Can't miss that." She thrust the plate toward him. "I'll come back later and get my dish."

After placing the parcel on the table nearby, he took the cinnamon rolls from his neighbor, their scent teasing that less than robust appetite. "Thanks, Miss Kime."

"Tsk. Tsk. Didn't I tell you to call me Marcella, young man? Your grandma and me were good friends. I miss her."

"So do I, Miss—I mean, Marcella."

When she had traversed the four steps to his sidewalk, Jake closed his front door, shutting out the world. With a sigh, he scanned his living room, the familiar surroundings where he controlled his environment, knew what to expect. Even Marcella's visits weren't surprises anymore.

Jake balanced the plate on the box, carried it into his office and set it on the desk to open later. It was from his father and his new wife— a care package as they'd promised in their last call. Finally, they weren't trying to talk him into coming to live with them in Florida anymore. He needed his space, and he certainly didn't want to be reminded daily that he'd let down the general—he wouldn't follow in his father's footsteps. He needed a sense of what this house had given when he was growing up—peace.

He snatched a cinnamon roll as he sat in front of his laptop, his coffee cup already on his right on a coaster. While he woke up his computer, he bit into the roll and closed his eyes, savoring the delectable pastry. Marcella sure could bake. Before getting started in his course work for his Ph.D. in psychology, he clicked on his email, expecting one from his doctor at the VA about some test results.

Only one email that wasn't junk popped up. He recognized the name, a message from the wife of a soldier who had served under him in Afghanistan. His heartbeat picked up speed. He should open it, but after an email a couple of weeks prior where he discovered one of his men had died from his injuries in an ambush, he didn't know if he could.

His chest constricted. But the woman's name taunted him. With a fortifying breath, he clicked on the message. As their commanding officer, it was his duty to know what happened to his men, even if he couldn't do anything about it.

His comrade was going in for another operation to repair the damage from a bomb explosion. Her words whisked Jake back to that day six months ago that had changed his life. The sound of the blast rocked his mind as though he were in the middle of the melee all over again.

Sweat beaded on his forehead and rolled down his face. His hands shook as he closed the laptop, hoping that would stop the flood of memories. He never wanted to remember that day. Ever. The walls of his home office began to close in on him, mocking what peace he felt in his familiar surroundings. He surged to his feet and hobbled around the room, dragging in breaths that didn't satisfy his need for oxygen.

I'm in Cimarron City. In my house. Safe.

In the midst of the terror that day in the mountain village, he'd grasped on to the Lord and held tight as He guided him through the rubble and smoke to save whomever he could. But where was God now when he needed Him? He felt abandoned, left to piece his life together. Alone.

He paced the room, glancing back at the computer a couple of times until he forced himself to look away. Lightheaded, he stopped at the window, leaning on his cane, and focused on his front lawn. Reconnoitering the area. Old habits didn't die easily.

He started to turn away when something out of the corner of his eye caught his attention. He swung back and homed in on a group of kids across the street—two boys beating up a smaller child.

Anger clenched his gut. He balled his hands as another kid jumped in on the lopsided fight. That clinched it for Jake. He couldn't stand by and watch a child being hurt. Adrenaline began pumping through him as though he were going into battle, pushing his earlier panic into the background. He rushed toward the front door. But out on his porch, anxiety slammed into his chest, rooting him to the spot.

Jake's gaze latched on to the three boys against the one, taking turns punching the child. All his thoughts centered on the defenseless kid, trying to protect himself. Heart pounding, Jake took one step, then another. His whole body felt primed to fight as it had when as a soldier he vied with the other part of him—sweat coating his skin, hands trembling, gut churning.

No choice.

Furiously he increased his pace until he half ran and half limped toward the group, pain zipping up his injured leg. The boys were too intent on their prey to notice him. When he came to a halt, dropping his cane, he jerked first one then another off the child on the ground. He tried holding on to the one he pegged as the leader while reaching for the third kid, but the boy yanked free and raced deeper into the park with the second one hurrying after him.

"What's your name?" Pain radiating up his bad leg, Jake blocked it as much as he could from his mind and clasped the arm of the last child, smaller than the other two who'd fled and more the size of the boy on the ground.

The assailant glared at him, his mouth pinched in a hard line.

The downed kid still lay huddled in a tight ball. As much as Jake wanted to interrogate the bully he held, he needed to see to the hurt child. He memorized the features of the third attacker then released him. As expected, the third attacker fled in the same direction as his cohorts.

That was okay. Jake could identify him. He wouldn't get off scot-free.

Adrenaline still surging, Jake knelt by the boy. That sent another sharp streak of pain up his thigh. But over the months he'd learned that if he concentrated hard enough, he could ignore the aches his injury still caused. "You're safe now. Can I help you? Where do you hurt?"

For a long moment the child didn't say anything. Didn't move.

Concern flooded Jake. He settled his hand on the boy's shoulder. "Where do you live? Can you make it home?" Should he call 911? Had the bullies done worse damage than he realized?

Slowly, the child uncurled his body. He winced as he turned and looked up. Jake took in the cut lip and cheek, blood oozing from the wounds, the eye that would blacken by tomorrow, the torn shirt.

"Let me help you home."

Wariness entered the kid's blue eyes. "I'm fine." He swiped his dirty sleeve across his mouth, smearing the blood.

"Who were those guys?"

The child clamped his lips together, cringing, but keeping his mouth closed.

"The least I can do is make sure you get home without those kids bothering you again."

The boy's eyes widened.

"Okay?"

The child nodded once then tried to stand. Halfway up, his legs gave out, and he sank to the ground.

Jake moved closer. "Let me help." He steadied himself with his cane.

When the boy stood with Jake's assistance, he wobbled but remained on his feet.

"I've been in a few fights. I know you have to get your bearings before doing too much."

The child tilted his head back and looked up at Jake, pain reflected in his eyes. "Did ya win?"

"Sometimes. Can you walk home? If you don't think you can, I'll call your parents." He dug into his pocket and pulled out his cell phone.

"No, I can walk." The child glanced over his shoulder. "Do you think they'll come back?"

"Not if they know what's good for them. I won't let them hurt you again."

"I wish that was true," the boy, probably no more than ten, mumbled, his head dropping. His body language shouted defeat.

"It's getting worse," Jake heard the kid mumble to himself. That again aroused the protective instinct in him.

"C'mon. Show me where you live. Is it far?" He looked back to check for the trio who had jumped the child. A male jogger and a couple, hands clasped, were the only people he saw in the park. "I'm Jake. What's your name?" With his injured leg throbbing, he used his cane to support more of his weight than usual.

"Josh." The boy dragged his feet as they turned the corner onto Sooner Road.

"Why were those kids bothering you?" The question came out before Jake could censor himself. He didn't want to get involved. Yet, the second he took the first step toward the fight, he had become involved, knowing firsthand what the boy was going through.

Josh mumbled something again, but Jake could hear only the words, "like to fight."

"Have those guys bullied you before?"

The boy's pace slowed until he came to a stop

in front of a one-story, redbrick house with a long porch across the front. "Yeah. The big one has since he moved here," he said, his head still hanging.

"Do your parents know?" Jake studied the top of the child's head, some blood clotted in the brown hair. The urge to check the wound inundated him. He started to bring his hand up.

Josh jerked his chin up, anger carved into his features while his eyes glistened. "I don't have a dad. I don't want my mom knowing. You can't tell her." He took a step back. His hands fisted at his sides as if he were ready to defend that statement.

"I won't."

The taut set of the child's shoulders relaxed some, his fingers flexed.

"But *you* will."

"No, I won't. I can take care of this myself. Mom will just get all upset and worried."

"She'll know something is wrong with one look at you." Jake gestured toward the house with a neatly trimmed yard, mums in full bloom in the flower bed and an inviting porch with white wicker furniture, perfect for enjoying a fall evening. Idyllic, as if part of the world wasn't falling apart with people battling each other. "Is this where you live?"

Josh stuck his lower lip out and crossed his arms, wearing a defiant expression.

Instantly, Jake flashed back to an incident with a captive prisoner who gave him that same look. His heartbeat raced. His breathing became shallow. His world shrank to that small hut in the mountains as he faced an enemy who had been responsible for killing civilians and soldiers the day before. He felt the shaking start in his hands. Jake fought to shut down the helplessness before it took over.

"Josh, what's going on?" A female voice penetrated the haze of memories.

Jake blinked and looked toward the porch. A tall woman, a few inches shy of six feet, with long blond hair pulled back in a ponytail that swished, marched down the steps toward them, distress stamped on her features.

"What happened to you?" Stooping in front of the boy, the lady grasped Josh's arms. When he didn't say anything, she peered up at Jake. "What happened?"

"Is Josh your son?"

"Yes." The anxiety in her blue eyes, the same crystalline color as the boy's, pleaded for him to answer the question.

Jake shifted. He'd done what he said he would do. He'd delivered the child safely home. It was time to leave Josh and his mother to hash out what had occurred in the park. He backed away, his grip on the cane like a clamp. He spied the imploring look in Josh's eyes. "Your son needs to tell you," he said.

She turned back to the boy. "You're bleeding, your eye is red and your clothes are a mess. Did you get in a fight?"

The boy nodded.

"Why? That's not you, Josh."

The kid yanked away from his mom and yelled, "Yeah! That's the problem!" He stormed toward the house.

Jake took another step back.

She whirled toward him, her face full of a mother's wrath. "What's going on?"

"He was in a fight."

"I got that much from him."

"I broke it up and walked him home." Jake could barely manage his own life. He didn't want to get in the middle of someone else's, but the appeal in Josh's mother's eyes demanded he say something. "Three boys were beating up Josh."

"Why?"

"That you have to ask him. I came in after it started, and he wasn't forthcoming about what was going on."

"But something is. I get the feeling this wasn't the first time."

"A good assumption."

"I'm Emma Langford." She paused, waiting for him to supply his name.

He clamped his teeth down hard for a few seconds before he muttered, "Jake Tanner. I live around the corner, across from the park." Why did he add the last? Because there was something in her expression that softened the armor around his heart.

The woman glanced up and down the street, kneading her fingertips into her temple. "I don't know what to do. It sounds like they ganged up on Josh. Have you seen them around?"

"No, but I know what they look like, especially one of them close to Josh's size. The other two were bigger than him. Maybe older." He could understand a mother's concern and the need to defend her child. He'd often felt the same way about the men under his command.

"So my child is being bullied." Weariness dripped from each word.

Jake moved closer, an urge to comfort assailing him. Taking him by surprise. For months he'd been trying to shut off his emotions. Hopelessness and fear were what had him in his current condition: unable to function the way he had before his last tour of duty.

"He never said a word to me, but I should have known," she said in a thick voice. "No wonder he's been so angry and withdrawn these past few months."

"That would be a good reason. Chances are he doesn't know how to handle it, either."

"Do you think they live in the neighborhood?" She panned the houses around her as if she could spot where the bullies lived.

"Maybe. They were in the park when the fight occurred."

"I need to find out who's bullying my son and put a stop to it."

"How?" Jake could remember being bullied in school when he was in the sixth grade.

"I don't know. Confront them. Have a conversation with their parents."

"Often that makes the situation worse. It did for me when I was a child." The reply came out before he could stop the words.

"But maybe it would put a stop to it. Make a difference for my son." Her forehead creased, she glanced back at the house. "I want to thank you for what you did for Josh. Would you like some tea or lemonade?"

He hesitated. He needed to say no, but he couldn't, not after glimpsing the lost look in the lady's eyes.

"Please. I make freshly squeezed lemonade." She started toward her house. "We can enjoy it outside on the porch."

Part of him wanted to follow her, to help her—

the old Jake—but that guy was gone, left in the mountains where some of his men had died.

She slowed and glanced back, anxiety shadowing her eyes. "I'm at a loss about what to do. Tell me what happened to you when you were bullied. That is, if you don't mind. It may help me figure out what to do about Josh."

It was just her porch. He wouldn't be confined. He could escape easily.

He took a step toward her, then another, but with each pace closer to the house, his legs became heavier. By the time he mounted the stairs, he could barely lift them. He paused several feet from the front door and glanced at the white wicker furniture, a swing hanging from the ceiling at the far end. Thoughts of his mother's parents' farmhouse where he'd spent time every summer came to mind. For a moment peace descended. He tried to hold on to that feeling, but it evaporated in seconds at the sound of an engine revving and then a car speeding down the street.

The sudden loudness of the noise made him start to duck behind a wicker chair a couple of feet away. He stopped himself, but not before anger and frustration swamped him. His heartbeat revved like the vehicle, and the shakes accosted him. He clasped his hands on the knob of his cane and pressed it down into the wooden slat of the porch.

What was he thinking? He should never have accepted her invitation.

"I'm sorry. I can't. I have stuff to do at home." He pivoted so fast he nearly lost his balance and had to bring his cane down quickly to prevent it.

"Thank you for your help today with my son," Emma quickly got out.

Sweat popped out on his forehead and ran down his face, into his eyes. He concentrated on the stinging sensation to take his mind off everything rushing toward him. As fast as his injured leg would let him, he hurried toward his house and the familiar surroundings where he knew what to expect. The trembling in his hands had spread throughout his body by the time he arrived in his yard.

Once inside his home, he fell back against the door and closed his eyes, trying to slow his stampeding heartbeat. His chest rose and fell rapidly as he gulped air. He slid down the length of the door and sat on the tiled foyer floor, blocking the deep ache that emanated from his recent injury.

Rage at himself, at his situation swamped him, and he slammed his fist into his palm. Pain shot up his arm. He didn't care. It wasn't anything compared to how he hated what was happening to him.

What are You doing, God? I want a normal life. Not be a slave to these panic attacks. Why aren't You answering my prayers?

Chapter Two

From the front porch, Emma watched Jake Tanner limp down the sidewalk toward the corner at Park Avenue. Mr. Tanner had saved her son from getting hurt worse than he already was. Had the situation with Josh brought back bad memories of the man's childhood? Was that why he'd left so quickly? Why there was a poignant look in his dark brown eyes? She guessed she shouldn't have asked him about what happened to him when he was bullied. That couldn't be easy for anyone to remember.

Mr. Tanner rounded the corner and disappeared from her view. From what she'd seen of the man, it certainly appeared he could take care of himself, even with his injured leg. She was five feet ten inches, and he had to be a good half a foot taller. He might be limping but clearly that didn't stop him from doing some kind of physical exercise. Dressed in tight jeans and a black T-shirt, he looked well built with a hard, muscular body—a little leaner than he was probably accustomed to.

"Jake Tanner" rolled off her tongue as if she'd said it before. Why did it sound familiar to her? Where had she heard his name? Had she run into him somewhere in town? She wasn't from Cimarron City but had lived here for years. But then he would be a hard man to forget with his striking good looks.

Had he hurt himself recently? Was the injury to his left leg permanent? Questions began to flood her mind until she shook her head.

No. He made it clear he'd helped Josh, but that was all. Besides, she had her hands full with a child who was angry all the time. And there were her two jobs—one as a veterinary assistant at Harris Animal Hospital and the other as a trainer for service dogs with the Caring Canines Foundation with Abbey Winters, her best friend. Abbey had founded the organization that placed service and therapy dogs with people who needed them. Emma didn't want any more complications in her life, and she certainly wasn't interested in dating, even though it had been three years since her husband died, leaving her widowed at twenty-nine with a son.

Who is my top priority—Josh.

Emma threw one last glance at the corner of Sooner and Park, then headed inside and toward

Josh's bedroom. They needed to have a conversation about what had happened today whether her son wanted to talk or not. Her child would not be used as a punching bag. The very thought tightened her chest and made breathing difficult.

She halted outside his closed door, drew air into her lungs until her nerves settled and then knocked. She half expected Josh to ignore her, but thirty seconds later, he swung open the door. A scowl puckered his face, and he clenched his jaw so tightly, a muscle in his cheek twitched, underscoring his anger. He left her standing in the entrance, trudged to his bed and flung himself on his back onto his navy blue coverlet.

"I'm not telling you who those guys are."

"Why not?" She moved into his room and sat at the end of the bed, facing him.

"You'll say something to them or their parents."

"Are you being bothered at school? Is that why you haven't wanted to go these past six weeks since school started?"

He clamped his lips together until his mouth was a thin, tight line.

"I'm going to talk to your teacher whether you say anything or not. I can't sit by and let someone, or in this case, several boys bully you."

"Don't, Mom. I'll take care of this. It's *my* problem."

The sheen in Josh's eyes, the plea in his voice

tore at her composure. She wanted to pull him into her arms and never let go—to keep him safe with her. *Sam, I need you. This is what a dad handles with a son. What do I do?*

She'd never felt so alone as at this moment, staring at Josh fighting the tears welling in his eyes. "I know Mrs. Alexander would want to know. Every child should be safe at school. This is not negotiable. I can't force you to tell me, but I need to know who is doing this to you."

"I'm not a snitch. That's what they'll call me. I'll never live it down."

"So what's your plan? Let them keep beating you up? What if Mr. Tanner hadn't seen them and stopped them? What do you think would have happened?"

Josh shrugged, turned away from her and lay on his bed.

Emma remembered Jake Tanner's words about how talking with the bullies' parents sometimes only made the situation worse. Then what should she do? What could Josh do? "At least make sure you have friends around you. Don't go anywhere alone. It's obvious now you can't go to Craig's house through the park. I'll have to drive you to and from your friends' houses. I'll pick you up from school and take you in the morning. I'll talk to Dr. Harris and figure out a way to do that with my work schedule. If I can't, I'll see if Abbey will.

She takes Madi to and from school." As she listed what she would do, she realized all those precautions weren't really a solution.

Then in the meantime, she'd talk to the school about the bullying. She had to do something to end this. The thought of her son hurting, physically and emotionally, stiffened her resolve to help him somehow whether he liked it or not. She hated that bullies were almost holding her son hostage.

"Don't say anything to Mrs. Alexander, Mom."

Emma rose and hovered over Josh. "I have to. It's my job as your parent. I can't ignore what happened."

He glared at her. "I hate you. You're going to make my life miserable."

The words hurt, but she understood where they came from—fear and anger at his situation. She knew those feelings well, having experienced them after Sam passed away. "I love you, Josh, and your life right now with these bullies isn't what you want or deserve."

Her son buried his head under his pillow.

"I need to check your cuts and clean them."

"Go away."

"I'm not leaving. You aren't alone."

He tossed the pillow toward the end of the bed. "I wish Mr. Tanner hadn't interfered. Then you wouldn't be making such a big deal out of this."

"Thankfully he did, and believe me, I would

have made a big deal out of it when I saw you in this condition whether he'd stepped in or not. I'll be right back with the first-aid kit."

Josh grumbled something she couldn't hear.

As she gathered up what she needed, a picture of Jake Tanner flashed into her mind. Short, dark hair—military style like her brother's... Emma snapped her fingers. That was it. Ben had mentioned a Jake Tanner on several occasions because he was the army captain Ben had served under in his Special Forces Unit. Could this be the same man?

After she patched up an uncooperative Josh, she left him in his bedroom to pout. When she really thought about Josh's angry behavior and keeping to himself, she realized it had begun during the summer. She'd hoped his mood would improve when school started and he saw his friends more. But it hadn't. She'd tried talking to him. He'd been closemouthed and dismissive of her concerns. Why hadn't she seen it earlier?

She made her way to the kitchen to start lunch but first decided to call her brother. She knew it would nag her not to know whether the Jake Tanner she'd met was Ben's company's commanding officer. She remembered Ben's commenting they both had lived in Oklahoma so it was possible.

She called his cell phone number. "Hi, bro. Do you have a moment to appease my curiosity?"

Emma leaned against the kitchen counter, staring out the window over the sink at the leaves beginning to change colors.

"For you, always. What's going on?"

"Josh was in the park and some boys jumped him and beat him up. Apparently, this wasn't the first time they'd approached him."

"How's Josh?"

"Some cuts and bruises but I think his self-confidence is more damaged than anything."

"I wish I didn't live so far away. I could help him. With my new job I'm working weekends, so that doesn't leave a lot of time to even drive to Cimarron City when Josh isn't in school."

She didn't want Ben to feel this was his problem. He lived in Tulsa and was just getting his life back. "I'm going to talk to the school on Monday about it. But that's not what I wanted to speak with you about. A man named Jake Tanner broke up the fight and brought Josh home. He lives across the street from where it happened on Park Avenue. Could he be your captain? You said something about his living around here once. Am I crazy to even think it could be the same guy?" And why in the world did it make a difference, except that it would bug her until she found out?

"So that's where he is. Some of my buddies from the old company who made it back were wondering where he went when he was let out of the army hospital a few months ago. He has an email address but hasn't said where he is when he's corresponded with any of the guys. I've been worried. I should have thought about Cimarron City. He lived there for a while when his father was stationed at the army base nearby. And he used to visit his grandmother there in the summer. I think his grandmother died last year, but I thought since his father is stationed in Florida, that might be where he went."

"What happened to him?"

"I was stateside when my old company was ambushed and about a quarter of the men were killed, many others injured. Captain Tanner was one of them. A bullet in his left leg. Tore it up. I hear he almost lost it."

She recalled how emotionally messed up Ben had been last year when he was first released from the military hospital and honorably discharged from the army. He didn't have a job then—couldn't hold one down—and lived with their parents in Tulsa.

"How did he seem to you?"

"He couldn't get away fast enough. I invited him to share a drink for rescuing Josh, and he backed away as if I was contagious."

"What did you say to him?" Half amusement, half concern came over the line from her brother.

"Nothing. He wasn't mad at me. He was—"

she searched her mind for a word to describe the earlier encounter "—vulnerable. Something was wrong. Maybe his leg was hurting or something like that. I did see his hands shaking. He tried to hide it, and he was breathing hard, sweating. That didn't start really until he'd been talking to me for a while. Do you think it could be…" She wasn't a doctor and had no business diagnosing a person.

"Post traumatic stress disorder?"

Ben had recovered from his physical injuries within months of returning stateside, but what had lingered and brought her brother to his knees was PTSD. Last year she'd trained her first service dog to help her brother deal with the effects of the disorder. "How's Butch doing?"

"He's great. You don't know how much he changed my life for the better."

Yes, she did. She saw her brother go from almost retreating totally from life to now holding down a job and functioning normally. He still lived with their parents, but she'd heard from her mom he was looking for his own apartment. "Are you having any problems?"

"Yes, occasionally, but Butch is right there for me. I can't thank you enough for him. Do you think you could pay Captain Tanner a visit? See how he is? I know what happened to him was bad, and as tough as he was, I wouldn't be surprised if he's dealing with PTSD. It can take out the strongest people."

Like Ben. He'd been a sergeant with an Army Special Forces Unit with lethal skills she couldn't even imagine. Yet none of that mattered in the end.

"Please, sis. I owe Captain Tanner my life. He pulled me out of the firefight that took me down. If he hadn't, I would have died."

"What if it isn't your Captain Tanner?"

"Was the person six and a half feet, dark brown hair, built like a tank, solid, with dark eyes—almost black?"

"That's him." She thought of the man she'd met today and realized she owed him, too. Not only for Ben but Josh. "I'll go see him. What do you want me to do?"

As her brother told her, she visualized Jake Tanner. The glimpse of anguish she'd seen in those dark eyes haunted her. He'd been quick to disguise it until the end when he started backing away from her. That black gaze pierced straight through her heart, and she doubted he even realized what he'd telegraphed to her—he was a man in pain.

The following Tuesday, Emma brought a terrier on a leash into the back room of the Harris Animal Hospital where she worked for Dr. Harris, the father of her best friend, Abbey Winters.

"I think this gal will be great to train as a service dog. She's smart and eager."

"Even tempered?" Abbey, her partner in the Caring Canines Foundation, asked as she looked at the medium-size dog with fur that was various shades of brown.

"Surprisingly calm. That combined with this breed's determination and devotion can make a good service dog."

"I'll take her out to Caring Canines since you're working with the German shepherd at your house." The kennel and training facilities of the organization were housed at Winter Haven Ranch where Abbey lived with her husband, Dominic.

"Shep will make a good service dog, too. I've even got a possible owner for him. You know I've been doing the same training with Shep as I did with Butch."

"How is your brother?"

"Doing so much better. I talked to Ben twice this past weekend."

Abbey's eyebrows lifted. "That's unusual. Doesn't your brother hate talking on the phone?"

"Yeah, he prefers video chatting where he can see a person's face, and the second time that's what we did. I got to see Butch. Ben looks better each time I see him. Butch has been good for my brother, and if what Ben thinks is true, Shep will be good for Captain Tanner."

"Another soldier? Is it a physical injury? PTSD?"

"Both. When those kids I told you about yesterday jumped Josh, Captain Tanner was the man who rescued him. After he left my house Saturday, I couldn't shake the feeling I'd heard that name somewhere. I finally remembered Ben served under a Captain Jake Tanner."

"So you called your brother to find out. I know how you are when you get something in your head. You don't give up until you find out the truth."

Emma laughed. "You've nailed me. I called him to see. Ben did some checking around after we talked on Saturday and found out that Captain Tanner has basically withdrawn into his house. Ben has a few connections, and one thought the captain was suffering from PTSD, although he doesn't seem to be participating in any therapy groups through the VA."

"How does Captain Tanner feel about having a service dog?"

"I don't know. I only talked to him that one time. I plan on taking him some brownies as a thank-you for helping Josh. Shep will go with me. I'll introduce him to the idea of a service dog slowly."

She wasn't sure if Jake Tanner would even open the door. She'd use the excuse she needed more information about the three boys who attacked Josh. Not only did she want to help the captain if he was suffering from PTSD, but she did need descriptions of the boys to give her an idea who could be bullying Josh. His teacher had requested any information to help her with the situation at school.

"Shep could help him, but he needs counseling, too. Maybe he's getting private therapy."

"Possibly, but Ben doesn't think so from what he's hearing from his army buddies in the area. Do you have room in your PTSD group?" Though Emma's best friend ran the Caring Canines Foundation, she still conducted a few counseling groups.

"If he'll come, I'll make room. The members are there to support each other, and talking about it has helped them. But there aren't any soldiers in the group."

"Maybe you should start one for people who have been bullied." Josh was dealing with some of the same symptoms as someone with PTSD—anger, anxiety and depression.

"If I only had more time in the day. Even quitting work at the hospital hasn't changed much because I'm training more dogs now. There is such a demand for them. So you didn't get any answers about who's bullying Josh from your meeting with Mrs. Alexander yesterday?"

"She hasn't seen anything, and since I didn't know the bullies' names and couldn't describe them, there wasn't much she could do but keep an eye out for any trouble. Most of the boys in his class are bigger than Josh, so the bullies could be in Mrs. Alexander's room. Or from the other fifth-grade classes."

"They could even be sixth-graders. It was a good idea to get him off the bus. It's hard for the driver to keep an eye on the road and what students are doing at the same time." Abbey leaned down and stroked the terrier. "Did Dad give his okay on this dog?"

Emma nodded. "Your father checked her over and she's medically sound. It's Madi's turn to name the dog. Let me know what she chooses." Madi was Abbey's ten-year-old sister-in-law whom she and Dominic were raising.

"Madi takes her job as name giver very seriously. She'll stew on it for days," Abbey said with a chuckle.

"Not too long. I want to start right away and a name helps. Now that I'm winding down with Shep, I have a slot open." Since she still worked full-time at the animal hospital, she could train only one dog at a time.

Abbey took the leash from Emma. "Good. Before long we're going to need another trainer, or you're going to have to quit your job here."

"Your father might have something to say about that. I'm going to look at training more than one dog. Hopefully that will help."

"I know, but the requests for free service dogs have increased over the past few months, especially now that veterans have heard about our foundation and the VA has stopped paying for service dogs. Many of the veterans can't afford an animal from the agencies that charge for them."

"How are the donations coming?" Emma leaned against the exam table, the terrier rubbing against her leg.

"They're increasing. My husband is very good at helping to raise money for Caring Canines. Dominic can attest to the good a dog can bring to a person after how Madi responded to Cottonball following her surgery to help her walk again."

Emma smiled. "And now Madi is running everywhere. You wouldn't know she had been in a plane crash twenty months ago."

"She's telling me she wants to learn to train dogs. I'm having her shadow me."

"A trainer in the making. There was a time I thought Josh would want to train dogs, but lately nothing interests him."

A frown slashed across Abbey's face. "Because he's too busy dodging the bullies after him."

"I know God wants me to forgive the boys, but I'm not sure I can. Josh has already had to deal with losing his dad. They were very close."

"Madi needed a woman's influence, and I

suspect Josh could benefit from a male being in his life."

"He has Ben when he comes to visit."

"You don't want to get married again?" Abbey started for the reception area of the animal hospital, leading the terrier on a leash.

Emma followed her down the hallway. "I know you found love with Dominic, but Sam gave me everything I needed. I've had my time." Abbey had loved her husband so much that when he'd died, it had left a big hole in her heart she didn't think any man could fill.

"That's wonderful, but he's been gone for three years. I realized when I met and fell in love with Dominic that we could have second chances, and they can work out beautifully."

"Says a lady madly in love with her husband. When am I going to fit a man into my life with work, training dogs and raising Josh?"

"When your heart is ready," Abbey said. They stood at the entrance into the reception area where a client waited with her cat. Abbey winked at Emma and started toward the main door. "See you later at the ranch."

"I'll be there today, but tomorrow I'm going to be busy baking brownies and scouting out the situation with Captain Tanner. At the very least, my brother wants a report he's okay. And if Captain

Tanner needs Shep, I'll do my best to persuade him of the benefits of a service dog."

At the door Abbey turned back and answered, "He may need more than Shep. Animal companionship is great but so is human companionship." She gave a saucy grin then left.

Emma faced the receptionist and lady in the waiting room. "Ignore what that woman said. She doesn't know what she's talking about." Emma turned and headed for exam room one to prepare it for the next client. The sound of chuckles followed her down the hallway, and heat reddened her cheeks.

On Wednesday, Jake's hand shook as he reread the letter from the army. He was being awarded the Distinguished Service Medal for his heroic actions in the mountains in Afghanistan.

Why? I'm no hero. Not everyone came home. Those left behind are the true heroes.

Guilt mingled with despair as he fought to keep the memories locked away. The bombs exploding. The peppering of gunfire. The screams and cries. The stench of death and gunpowder.

The letter slipped from his hand and floated to the floor. He couldn't protect all his men. He'd tried. But he'd lost too many. Friends. Battle buddies.

He hung his head and his gaze latched on to

the letter. Squeezing his eyes shut, he still heard in his mind the words General Hatchback would say when he gave him the medal during the Veterans Day Ceremony—six weeks away. And no doubt, his father would be there.

No, he wouldn't go. He didn't deserve it. He'd done his duty. He didn't want a medal for that. He just wanted to be left alone.

The doorbell chimed, startling him. He jerked his head up and looked toward the foyer. He went to the window and saw the delivery guy from the grocery store. Using his cane, he covered the distance to the door at a quick pace and let the young man in.

"Hi, Mr. Tanner. I'll put these on the counter in your kitchen."

While Morgan took the sacks into that room, Jake retrieved his wallet from his bedroom and pulled out some money for a tip then met the guy in the foyer. "Thanks. See you a week from tomorrow."

"I'm off next Thursday. A big game at school. Got to support our Trojans."

"When will you be working next week?" Jake handed him the tip.

"Friday afternoon and evening." Morgan stuffed the money into his pocket.

"Then I'll call my order in for that day."

"You don't have to. Steve delivers when I don't."

Jake put his hand on the knob. "That's okay. Friday is fine. I'll have enough to tide me over until then." He was used to Morgan. The young man did a good job, even putting his meat and milk into the refrigerator for him. He didn't want a stranger here. Jake swung the front door open for Morgan to leave.

"Sure, if that's what you want." The teen left.

When Jake moved to close the door behind Morgan, he caught sight of Emma and a black and brown German shepherd coming up the sidewalk. He couldn't very well act as if he wasn't home, and there was no way he would hurt her by ignoring the bell since she'd seen him. But company was not what he wanted to deal with at the moment.

Then his gaze caught the smile that encompassed her face, dimpling her cheeks and adding sparkle to her sky-blue eyes as though a light shone through them. He couldn't tell her to go home. He'd see her for a few minutes then plead work, which was true. He had a paper due for his doctorate program.

"Hi. How are you doing today?" Emma stopped in front of him, presenting him with a plate covered with aluminum foil. "I brought a thank-you gift. Brownies—the thick, chewy kind. I hope you like chocolate."

"Love it. How did you know?"

"Most people do, so I thought it was a safe dessert to make for you. I love to bake and this is one of my specialties."

"Thanks. You and my neighbor ought to get together. Marcella is always baking," he said, with the corners of his mouth twitching into a grin, her own smile affecting him.

"And bringing you some of it?"

"Yes." He stared into her cheerful expression and wanted to shout there was nothing to be upbeat about, but something nipped his negative thoughts—at least temporarily. Her bright gaze captured him and held him in its grasp.

Since Saturday, he'd been plagued with memories of their meeting that day. He'd even considered going to her house and seeing how Josh was. He only got a couple of feet from his porch before he turned around. They were strangers, and she didn't need to be saddled with a man—even as a friend—who was crippled physically and emotionally.

Jake stepped away from the entrance. "Come in. I have to put away the rest of my groceries." For a few seconds, panic unfolded deep inside him. He was out of practice carrying on a normal conversation with a civilian after so many years in war-conflicted areas. Sucking in a deep breath, he shoved the anxiety down.

As she passed him, a whiff of her flowery scent wafted to him—lavender. His mother used to wear it. For a few seconds he was thrust into the past. He remembered coming into the kitchen when his mom took a pan of brownies out of the oven. The aromas of chocolate and lavender competed for dominance in his thoughts, and a sense of comfort engulfed him.

Emma turned toward him with that smile still gracing her full mouth. It drew him toward her, stirring other feelings in him. He'd had so little joy in his life lately. That had to be the reason he responded to a simple grin.

"It's this way." He limped ahead of her through the dining room and into the kitchen.

"I like this." Emma put the plate on the center island counter. "It's cozy and warm. Do you cook?"

"No, unless you call *cooking* opening a can and heating up whatever is in it. My meals aren't elaborate. A lot of frozen dinners." Jake's gaze landed on the German shepherd. *Beautiful dog to go with a beautiful woman, but why did she bring the animal with her?* Had his strange behavior the other day scared her somehow? When a panic attack took hold of him, it was hard for him to do much about it, which only made the situation worse.

"That's a shame. You need to come to my house one evening. I love to cook when I have the time."

"What keeps you so busy you can't cook very often?" Jake asked, resolved to stay away from any topic about him as he began emptying the sacks on the countertop. Focus on her. A much safer subject to discuss.

"Training dogs, working a full-time job at the animal hospital and trying to raise a child who's giving me fits."

"Things aren't any better?"

"No. The Cold War has been declared at my house. He didn't appreciate my talking to his teacher."

Jake whistled. "Yep, that will do it."

"Are you taking his side? Are you saying I shouldn't have talked with his teacher about his being bullied?"

Jake threw up his hands, palms outward. "Hold it right there. I am not taking anyone's side. That's between you and your son."

"I could use your help with this situation."

He scanned the room, looking for a way out of the kitchen and this conversation. He didn't want to be in the middle between a mother and son. "I don't know the boys who ganged up on Josh."

"But you saw them. Can you describe the culprits? Even one of them?"

"Maybe the smallest kid. Brown hair, brown eyes."

"Good. Do you have a piece of paper and a pencil?"

"Yes, but…" Staring at the determination in

Emma's expression, he realized the quickest way to get rid of her was to give her what she wanted—at least the little he knew. He crossed to the desk under the wall phone and withdrew the items requested.

Emma took them. "I love to draw. If you tell me what he looks like, I'll try to sketch a portrait of him. Brown hair and eyes as well as a small frame fit a lot of kids in Cimarron City. So let's start with what shape his face is—oval, oblong, heart shaped? Is his jaw square, pointy, round?"

Staring at the dog sitting near the back door, Jake rubbed his day-old beard stubble. He'd forgotten to shave this morning. He was doing that more lately. When he glanced down at his attire, he winced at the shabby T-shirt and jeans with several holes in them. If someone who didn't know him walked in right now, that person would think Jake was close to living on the street. Suddenly he saw himself through Emma's eyes. And he didn't like the picture.

The military had taught him always to be prepared and to keep himself presentable. Lately he'd forgotten his training. The least he could do was change clothing. He wouldn't shave because her visit was impromptu, and he didn't want to give her the wrong impression—that he cared. He knew better than to care, not with the upheaval in his life.

"Your visit has taken me by surprise. I'll be back in a minute." He gestured to the kitchen. "Make yourself at home. I have a large, fenced backyard if you want to put your pet outside. A big dog like that probably requires a lot of exercise." He wanted to add: *I won't hurt you. I'm only hurting myself.*

"That's great."

As she walked to the back door, Jake slipped out of the kitchen and hurried to his bedroom. He felt encouraged she wasn't afraid of him since she was putting her German shepherd outside. Somehow he would beat what he was going through…but he didn't think he could by the time of the medal ceremony on Veterans Day.

After rummaging in his closet for something nicer to wear, he began to change. He caught sight of himself in the full-length mirror on the back of the door and froze. He didn't know the man staring back at him in the reflection. He sank onto his bed and plowed his fingers through his unruly hair.

I just want some hope, Lord.

Chapter Three

Jake hadn't kicked her out of his house yet. That was a good sign. Emma knew how much control meant to him right now because Ben had gone through a period where he tried to manage everything around him. He needed to know what was going to happen next. The trouble was life wasn't predictable, and that was where Ben had problems. He'd lost his patience and laid-back attitude, but in the past nine months he was getting them back. He was realizing finally that God was the one in control and He was always there to help him through. Did Jake believe in God?

After letting Shep out into Jake's backyard, Emma glanced around the neat kitchen, an olive-green-and-gold decor—no doubt his grandmother's touch when she lived in the house. She'd asked Marcella Kime, who went to her church, about Jake and this place. His grandmother had lived here until she died last year. The family hadn't sold it yet, so Jake must have decided to move in.

One sack of groceries was left on the counter. While she waited for Jake to return, she emptied the bag of food, then prowled the room. Maybe he skipped out the front door. When she heard a bark at the back one, she let Shep into the house.

She knelt and rubbed her hands along his thick black and brown fur. "I think the man is trying to send me a message," she whispered near the German shepherd's ear. "He doesn't know yet that I'm relentless when on a mission. He needs help and you. He's the reason Ben is alive. I owe Jake."

She nuzzled Shep, relishing the calmness that came from loving on the dog. In her house, there was always a dog she was training. With her full-time job, bringing a trainee home helped her to be around more if her son needed her. But the animal would eventually move on to another person. She'd found it easier not to have her own dog in case there were territorial issues when a new canine came for training. But maybe one day....

"Did he decide not to stay outside?"

Jake's question startled her, and she gasped. She swiveled around. "I didn't hear you come in."

"Sorry. I've learned to move quietly."

Emma straightened. "My husband made enough noise to alert the neighbors. Josh is just like his dad."

"What happened to your husband?"

"He died three years ago. He had epilepsy. It got worse over the years, and then he had a seizure he never recovered from." While on a ladder putting up Christmas lights because she had mentioned she wanted some. She'd intended for the teen next door to do the chore—not Sam. Guilt nibbled at her composure, and she shut it down. She was here to help Jake and possibly get some information concerning the kids bullying Josh.

"I'm sorry."

"Life has a way of changing and throwing you a curve when you least expect it."

He flinched. "Yeah, I know what you mean."

For a few heartbeats her gaze connected with his, and her stomach flip-flopped. The intensity in his look weakened her knees. She grasped the countertop.

As Jake moved to put away the canned goods and boxes from the last sack, she noted his change in clothing, trying to keep her attention somewhere besides those dark, compelling eyes. He still wore jeans but without any holes and a navy blue polo shirt. She saw his actions as a good sign. He wanted to look nicer for her, and that gave her hope.

"We can go into the living room, and I'll try to describe that last child I caught bullying Josh."

Emma retrieved the pad and pencil. "I appreciate it. I'm not sure what I'll do when I find out who the bullies are, but I need to know, if for no other reason than to help my son deal with the situation."

She went first toward the living area off the foyer. Shep walked beside her. Inside the room, she headed toward the couch. Her foot stepped on something, and she peered down. A sheet of paper—a letter? She picked it up as Jake entered. Her gaze lit upon the subject of the letter.

She swept around. "You're being awarded the Distinguished Service Medal. Congratulations!"

Jake stiffened. A thunderous expression descended over his features. He limped toward her and plucked the letter from her hands. "No reason to congratulate me because I survived when many didn't."

She eased onto the couch behind her, Shep sitting at her feet, close enough that she could stroke the back of his head and neck. She looked up into Jake's warring gaze as he skimmed the contents of the letter, then balled it up, crossed to the trash can and tossed it.

"They don't give the Distinguished Service Medal for being wounded. That's for serving your country above and beyond your normal duties. It's awarded for meritorious and heroic behavior. It's an honor you no doubt deserved."

"How would you know?"

She winced at his reproachful tone. "Because

my brother, Ben Spencer, told me what you did for him. You saved his life so I'm not surprised you're receiving the medal, one of the highest awarded by the government."

The color drained from his face. "You're Ben's sister?"

She nodded.

"How is he? I haven't had a chance to touch base…" The words faded into the quiet. Jake stared at his clasped hands. "I meant to see how he was once I was better."

"He's doing all right. His injuries are healed, and he's been coping with his PTSD. Making progress."

Jake lifted his head and gave her a searing look. "So what I heard is true? How's he dealing with it?"

She couldn't have asked for a better opening to talk about Shep. *Lord, give me the right words to say. This man is hurting.*

"Ben has a PTSD counseling group he attends in Tulsa, but he also has a service dog I trained for him. Butch has made a big difference in Ben's being able to go out and to participate in life without having so many panic attacks."

His eyebrows crunched together. "He's cured?"

"No, but the incidences he has are few, especially lately, and he's been able to work his way through them."

"I'm glad. He was a good soldier. I missed him when he returned home. Is he working?"

"Yes, at Gordon Matthews Industries as a computer programmer."

"Does he like it?"

"Yes, he's really enjoying it."

"That's good to hear. Sometimes it's hard to go back. A lot of men's lives have been messed up." Jake stared at the floor for a long moment, lost in thought.

Most likely remembering. The rigid set of Jake's shoulders made Emma wonder about his particular story. Each soldier had his own, some more traumatic than others. Ben had been flown back to the States eight months earlier due to his encounter with a land mine that had blown up a few feet from him in a field where one of his friends died. He lost part of his left arm while several other soldiers were also injured. But Ben kept in touch with many of the ones still in his old unit—there to help if they needed it. Jake wasn't staying in touch. Emma nudged Shep, giving him the signal to bark. He did.

Jake lifted his head, turning his attention toward the German shepherd. "He's a beautiful dog. How long have you had him?"

"Almost nine months. I've been training Shep to be a service dog. His specialty is working with people with PTSD." She watched Jake for a reaction.

He looked at her, a frown pulling his eyebrows down. "Why did you bring him today?"

"Because I like to take him out for a walk when I can and—" she swallowed to coat her dry throat "—I wanted you to meet him."

His eyes narrowed. "Why?"

Her gaze caught his. "Because I think you need a dog like Shep."

He rose, grappling for his cane. "I have work to do. Thank you for bringing the brownies." His hard expression shouted, *But don't ever come back!*

She didn't move. "Please. Let me explain."

He started to say something but pressed his lips together.

She took his silence as an okay. "I want to help you. I know what my brother went through when he came home. He couldn't hold down a job, even a simple one. He lived with our parents and didn't leave the house hardly at all—often holing himself up in his old bedroom. He got angry at the least little thing. He had the shakes and would shut down if something even little went wrong. He had nightmares and didn't want to sleep. When I gave him Butch, I saw how effective the dog was with him. Still is. Butch has a way of calming him down and centering him."

"That's your brother, not me." Jake took his seat again.

From checking with a few of his neighbors, Emma knew Jake rarely left his house. Jake Tanner was hiding out. Easier to stay home than go out in crowds where he had little control of what would happen around him. Ben had been like that at first. Butch had made the difference.

"I can help you if you'll just give Shep a chance."

"I'm capable of dealing with my problems. Healing takes time."

"A service dog can help that along."

"How? My injury was my leg. I'm up and about. I can walk now."

"There are other injuries that aren't so visible. A dog can help with those."

"What? Emotional ones?" He clasped his cane between his legs with both hands and leaned forward slightly.

"Yes. Dogs can sense when a problem is going to occur and intervene before it becomes worse."

His grip tightened around the ivory knob on the end of his cane until his knuckles whitened. "I've heard of other soldiers using service dogs. I don't want to have to care for an animal. I'm barely—" He snapped his mouth closed.

"What? Barely holding it together?" Emma asked, returning his unwavering gaze. She hadn't given up on Ben. Though they were virtual strangers, she could tell Jake needed help. She had promised her brother she would do what she could for his former commanding officer and she would, somehow.

Jake stiffened. "I have work to do."

She sighed. "Sometimes I can be too blunt. I'm sorry if I've upset you."

"I respect a person who speaks her mind, but that doesn't change the fact I don't need a service dog. I'm coping."

"That's good because Ben wasn't."

"It hasn't been that long since I came home. Recovery takes time." Jake's voice didn't sound as convincing as the man probably wanted.

"Time *and* help. I agree."

His gaze pinned her down. "I'm receiving help from my doctor."

Emma resisted the urge to squirm under his intense glare. "Is he here when you have panic attacks, flashbacks, nightmares?"

Jake winced, a mask falling into place as if he were shutting down all emotions.

The problem was a person couldn't block his feelings forever. They were there in the background, ready to strike when he least expected. Emma said, "A service dog can help a person with those kinds of things. When someone has a panic attack, the dog's trained to calm him. The animal can be trained to wake up a person who's having a nightmare. Flashbacks often lead to panic attacks or at the very least, emotional upheavals. A dog can be there at all hours to console, be a companion. Not to mention they're great listeners."

A tic twitched in his hardened jaw. "Does he talk back?"

Emma grinned. "I can do a lot with the dogs I train, but I haven't accomplished that yet. But they can understand a lot of commands, if properly taught. Shep has been trained in all those areas."

Jake stood. "Thanks for coming."

Jake's polite words and neutral expression didn't totally cover a hopelessness in his eyes. Emma could identify; she remembered how, when her husband died, she'd struggled to pay off his debts. She was still paying the hospital bill every month from the last time Sam was admitted.

Emma followed Jake from the living room. Shep trotted next to her. Ben's captain opened the front door and moved to the side to allow her to leave.

She stepped outside and pivoted. "Where did the boys attack Josh?"

He took two steps out onto the porch and pointed to the right near the wooded area. "There, and they fled into the trees. You didn't get around to doing the sketch of the small one."

"I've got another idea if you're willing."

His forehead wrinkled, wariness in his eyes. "What?"

"Josh has a yearbook from last year. Would you

be willing to look through it and see if you recognize any of the kids?"

"I'll try."

She smiled. "Great. I can bring it by tomorrow after work if that's okay."

He nodded, a solemn expression on his face.

"Then I'll see you around six."

She had started down the steps when he called out, "Tell Ben I'll be okay."

With a glance over her shoulder, she said, "You should call him and tell him yourself."

"I don't have his number."

"I can give it to you."

"Maybe tomorrow." He turned back into his house and shut the door.

As Emma walked home, she couldn't get Jake Tanner out of her mind. That haunted look in his dark eyes when she had talked about Ben's problems, and later what a service dog could be trained to do only reinforced in her mind that he needed help. Her brother had tried to deny it, too, and it had made things worse. She prayed Jake wouldn't. Tomorrow she had another chance to persuade him to try Shep.

The enemy surrounded Jake and what men he had left in the small mountain village, gunfire pelting them from all sides. The terrorists were closing in. He was trapped.

He signaled to his men to fall back into a house. He covered them as they made their way inside the shelter, then zigzagged toward it, seeking cover wherever he could. But as he ran toward the hut, it moved farther away from him. Escape taunted him. A safe haven just out of reach.

Someone lobbed a grenade that fell a few yards in front of him. He dived to the side, the explosion rocking him.

Crash!

Arms flailing, Jake shot straight up on the couch, blinking his eyes. He couldn't get enough air in his lungs. They burned. Everything before him twirled and swayed. He scrubbed his shaky hands down his sweat-drenched face, then drew in one deep inhalation then another. He folded in on himself, his arms hugging his chest, his head bent forward. Afraid even to close his eyes, he stared at his lap until his rapid heartbeat slowed. When the quaking eased, he looked up at his living room in Cimarron City. Not in a tent or hut in Afghanistan.

Safe. Quiet.

His gaze fell upon a lamp on the floor, shattered, along with a broken vase his grandma had cherished as a gift from his granddad. The sight of it destroyed what was left of his composure. His hands began to tremble more. Cold burrowed deep into his bones. He stuck them under his armpits.

Focus on the here and now. Not then. He shuffled through images in his mind until he latched on to one: Emma Langford, Ben's sister. He zeroed in on her light blue eyes, as bright as sunshine. He shifted his attention to her dazzling smile. He couldn't look away. The warmth of her expression chased away the chill.

He finally relaxed against the couch cushion. He couldn't believe he'd invited her back today. That realization earlier had driven him to take a short nap before she arrived since he hadn't slept much the night before. For that matter, since the nightmares began a couple of months ago, he slept only a few hours here and there.

He couldn't keep going like this, or he would stop functioning altogether. The very idea appalled him. In the army he'd been a leader of men who went into tough situations to protect and defend. Now he couldn't even leave his house without fearing he would have a panic attack and appear weak.

Lord, why? You brought me home to this—living in fear? How am I supposed to get better? What do I do?

His gaze returned to the mess on the floor, then trekked to the end table where the lamp and vase had been. He pushed to his feet to clean up the shattered pieces.

The chimes from the grandfather clock in the

foyer pealed six times. Emma would be here soon. He hobbled toward the kitchen and retrieved the broom and dustpan. The glass lamp was beyond repair. He swept the shards and tossed them into the trash can.

Then he turned his attention to the vase. His granddad had created pottery bowls and vases in his spare time. This was one of the few left. He picked up each piece and laid it on the end table, trying to decide if he could fix the vase with glue. Maybe it was possible with time and a steady hand.

The doorbell sounded, jolting his heartbeat to a quicker tempo. Emma. *She can't see this,* he thought, as though it were a symbol of his weakness. He opened the drawer on the end table and hurried to place what was left of the vase inside, then closed it.

It took him a minute to limp toward the foyer. Maybe she'd left. He hoped not, and that surprised him. When he opened the door, she stood on the porch with that warm smile and her hands full with a slender book and a plastic container.

"I'm sorry it took me so long to get to the door," was all he could think to say.

"I figured it would. You're still recovering from a leg injury. It might be a while before you're up for a jog." She stepped through his entrance. "I hope you don't mind, but I made beef stew this morning in the Crock-Pot and had plenty to share with you." She lifted the lid for him to see.

His stomach rumbled. The aroma filled his nostrils and made his mouth water. He'd had breakfast but skipped lunch. "How did you know I haven't eaten much today?"

"A lucky guess. I'll put this in your refrigerator, and you can heat it up when you feel like it." She walked toward his kitchen. Pausing at the entrance to his dining room, she looked back at him. "Then I'll show you the yearbook."

He started to follow her into the kitchen but decided not to and headed for the living room. "I'll be in here when you're through." He wanted to make sure there were no remnants of the broken vase or lamp on the floor.

After searching around the couch, he walked lamely to the leather chair with an ottoman. His left leg ached. He must have wrenched it when coming out of his nightmare. As he laid his cane on the floor by him, Emma came into the room. He lifted his leg onto the upholstered stool.

She took the couch, sitting at the end closest to him. "I'd heat it up in the microwave for about six minutes on high. I put bread in to bake, but it wasn't done when I left."

"You make your own bread?" Jake remembered his grandmother baking bread once a week, a good memory. "I used to love that smell when I was a kid and came to see Grandma."

"I'm not a coffee drinker, but I love to smell a pot percolating. As well as bacon frying and bread baking." She snapped her fingers. "Oh, the best smell I remember from my childhood is my mother baking a cherry pie. I loved to eat it with vanilla ice cream."

"If I wasn't hungry before you came, I am now."

"Good, you'll enjoy my stew." She rose and covered the short space between them. "This is the yearbook I was talking about."

He reached up to take it. Their fingers briefly touched, and his breath caught. He held it for a few extra seconds then released it slowly. Their gazes connected, and Emma paused as though not sure what to do.

He grinned, trying to dismiss the bond that sprang up between them for a moment. "Where's your German shepherd? I thought you'd bring him again."

She laughed, letting go of the yearbook, then sat on the couch. "I'll never force a dog on anyone, even when I think it would be good for him. Besides, Josh was throwing the Frisbee in the backyard for Shep, complaining that he was stuck at home and not at a friend's."

"Any problems with Josh in the past few days?"

"Nothing I can pin down. He tells me nothing more has happened, but he comes home from school angry and silent. I have to drag what little I can out of him."

"I remember those days when Mom tried to get me to tell her about my day at school, especially when the bullying was going on in the sixth grade."

"How did you handle it?"

"My mom found out and told my dad, who paid the parents of the instigator a visit. Tom Adams's parents didn't do anything to him, but Tom was furious at me. I won't ever forget his name. I did learn one thing. I learned to defend myself if I had to and to let others know I could take care of myself. Also, I made sure I was always with a group of friends. That way it was hard for Tom and his buddies to find me alone. They only attacked when I was by myself."

"Kids shouldn't have to worry about this. Did you have trouble at school?"

"Yes, especially at recess."

"Josh has been misbehaving so he doesn't go out for recess."

"Then it's probably happening at school. Some bullies can be very sneaky. They might even have a lookout."

Emma frowned. "When did the bullying stop?"

"Not until we moved here when I became

a seventh grader." He quirked a grin. "I also started growing over the summer and began to lift weights. I wanted to go out for football." He flipped open the yearbook. "How old is Josh?"

"Eleven."

"He's small for his age. I was, too."

Her eyes grew round. "But you're what, six-four or five now?"

"Yes. I shot up not long after I was Josh's age and used my size to help others who were bullied. Lifting weights helped me to bulk up. That's what I mean by looking as if I could take care of myself. My dad taught me some self-defense but stressed I should only use it if it was absolutely necessary. Telling Tom's parents didn't work at all. I think his dad was actually proud of his son for being big and tough."

"How can a parent…" Her tight voice trailed off into silence.

"I'm telling you what happened to me, so you'll be aware there could be a backlash. That course of action doesn't always take care of the problem."

Her shoulders slumped, and she stared at her lap. "This is when I wish my brother or father lived nearer."

"Maybe Ben can teach Josh some self-defense."

"You mean to fight back?"

"Not exactly. There are techniques he can use to protect himself from getting as hurt when he's outnumbered. One's to run as fast as he can. He needs to know it's okay to do that, and if he makes that decision, to do it right away or the first chance he gets. He needs to know he isn't a coward for running but smart for protecting himself. Also, a child who knows he can defend himself is more self-assured."

"My brother's going to be on the road for his job for the next month or so. And my father wouldn't know how. Not to mention he's frail."

Jake didn't have a reply to that. He didn't want to commit himself, not with the way his life was going. "You'll think of something," he said finally, realizing how lame that sounded. "Many bullies fight because they have low self-esteem. Make sure Josh knows that, and build him up. Bullies try to tear down others. It makes them feel superior. If Josh lets them know they can't do that, it might help."

She glanced up at him with that look that sent warm currents through him. "Will you have a talk with Josh and explain some of this to him? He won't listen to me."

Chapter Four

The seconds crawled by as Emma held her breath, waiting for Jake's answer.

His expression went blank, and he stared at his leg propped up on an ottoman. "All I can tell him is how I handled it. I don't know if that would work for him or not."

"I'll have you to dinner and you can talk to him. Anything you can tell him is better than nothing. He shuts me out. I don't know what else to do." She hated the desperate tone in her words.

"I can't come to your house for dinner. I don't want you going—"

"How about I bring the dinner here? I'll throw in fresh-baked bread, too."

Shaking his head, he chuckled. "You don't give up, do you?"

"No, stubborn is one of the traits I need to work on. When would you like me to bring dinner?"

He pressed his lips together, forming a tight, thin line, then said, "Do you work on Saturday?"

Hope flared in Emma. "I work at the Caring Canines Foundation until the early afternoon. Saturday night would be good for me. How about six-thirty?"

He nodded, then began looking through the pages of the yearbook. Halfway through the book, he tapped a picture. "That's the smallest one of the three."

Emma moved to glance over his shoulder at the photo. "Carson McNeil. He was in the same class last year with Josh. I don't think they're in the same one this year. His family goes to my church. Josh and Carson were friends at one time. I can't believe he's part of the group."

"Let me see if I can recognize the other two." Jake continued turning the pages and scanning each child until he pointed to another one in sixth grade.

She leaned forward to read the boy's name. "Sean Phillips. I haven't heard of him." She got a whiff of Jake's lime aftershave and pulled back, realizing how close she was to him. Her heart raced.

She retook her seat while he continued his search for the third kid. Catching herself staring at him, she dragged her attention away and scanned the living room, taking in the decor. Focusing on anything but the man across from her. As in the kitchen she saw his grandmother's touches in the knickknacks, a quilt thrown over the back of the couch and a myriad of pictures on the wall. She didn't see anything of Jake other than a photo of him on the wall in his dress uniform with his arm around his petite, white-haired grandma. Was this a place he would recuperate then move on?

The sound of Jake closing the book drew her away from her survey and back to him. "The third one wasn't in there?"

"Not that I could tell, but then I didn't get a good look at him. He was the first to run off."

"With Sean and Carson's names, I have something to go on."

"What do you plan to do?"

"I'm not sure. I guess I need to talk with these boys' parents, then see what happens." When his eyes darkened, she asked, "What would you do?"

He stiffened. All emotions fled his face.

"Never mind. I shouldn't have asked you. This isn't your problem." She started to rise.

Sighing, he waved her down. "Since you know Carson's family, I would start with him. But Josh needs to know what you're doing."

"I know. That's the part I dread more than talking to the parents. Why not Sean's? He's more likely the one behind the attack."

"I noticed he's older, in the sixth grade. You're

probably right. That means either he or the un-
known boy is the leader. Not Carson. You have a
better chance of getting something from Carson,
and since you go to the same church and know
his parents, they may step in." Jake massaged his
left thigh above the knee.

"I think so. Sandy McNeil and I are friends.
We've lost touch these past couple of years since
Carson and Josh aren't playing together the way
they used to, but I can't imagine her condoning
what her son's doing."

"But you can't say that about the other parents.
Start with the known first."

A clock somewhere in the house chimed seven
times. Emma glanced at her watch and bolted to
her feet. "I've overstayed my visit. I need to get
dinner on the table."

"I'm sure I'll enjoy my supper. It beats opening
a can of soup." Scooping up his cane, he struggled to stand.

As she watched him, she forced herself to remain still and not try to assist him. That would be
the last thing this man wanted. He needed to feel
he could do it on his own. But that didn't make the
urge to help any less strong. She was here because
of Ben, but she would stay because she wanted to.

At the front door, Emma waited until he came
nearer before saying, "Thanks for looking at the

photos. The more I know about what Josh is going through, the better I'm equipped to help him."

His features softened as he looked at her. "I hope everything goes okay when you talk to Josh about Carson and Sean. I doubt he'll be too happy."

"No, he'll be angry at me. But I'm his mother, and I'll do what I have to to protect him."

"He'll appreciate it one day."

"Just not today," Emma said with a grin. "We'll see you Saturday night." She turned to open the door but paused. "Oh, what do you like to eat?"

His eyes gleamed. "Surprise me."

"Then no big dislikes or allergies?"

"Nope. I do have one request."

Hand on knob, she glanced at him. "What?"

"Bring Shep with you."

Emma's mouth dropped open. Her large blue eyes fixed on Jake. Surprise flitted across her face. "You're going to take Shep?"

"I don't know. I'd like to see if we can get along first. If that's okay with you."

She grinned. "Sure. If you two don't connect, then he can't do his job. But I know you will. You won't regret it."

The sparkle in her gaze lured him toward her. "I have my doubts, but I hope you prove me wrong." After the last nightmare in a string of many, Jake had to do something. Here at home he could control a lot of his environment, but when he went to sleep, he couldn't choose his dreams. If a service dog could help him with that, great. If not, then at least he tried.

Sliding her hand into the pocket of her light jacket, Emma looked up. "I almost forgot. I've written Ben's number on this card for you. He wants you to call him when you're ready, and if you have any questions about a service dog, you can ask me or him."

Jake took the phone number, not sure if he would. "Thanks. See you Saturday."

"If you change your mind about picking something special to eat, my number's on the card, too. I won't shop until early Saturday afternoon."

He clasped the edge of the door as she moved out onto the porch. Her lavender scent lingered in the air. For a second he didn't want her to leave. She descended the steps and strolled down the sidewalk, stopping to wave to him. He waved back.

As he closed his door, he decided he wouldn't call Ben. It was one thing to admit he had a problem, but totally different to talk with someone about it. He wasn't there yet. Wasn't sure if he ever would be. He couldn't put what was happening to him in words, so how could he talk to anyone about it?

He was committed only to spending some time on Saturday night with the German shepherd, Emma and Josh. No more than that. Other than Marcella from next door and a few delivery people, no one else had been in this house until Emma. In less than a week, he'd seen her more than anyone lately.

He should keep his distance. He was in no condition to get involved with anyone, even as a friend. But while he didn't have much to give another, the thought of not seeing Emma on Saturday churned his gut.

On Saturday morning, Emma stood at the back door at the Caring Canines Foundation facilities and watched her son and Madi play with a few of the dogs in the fenced-in recreation area. A beautiful fall day still held a chill in the air, but the sun beamed down and would soon burn off the last of the fog rolling over Winter Haven Ranch.

"Josh is so good with the animals," Abbey said as she came up behind Emma.

"So is Madi. Maybe when we get old and gray, they'll take over the foundation."

"Don't forget Nicholas. He may be only a couple of months old, but he's already responding to the animals."

Abbey's son is such a happy baby. It made Emma want another child.

"Dominic and I have been talking about having another child soon so they'll be close in age. I want a little girl."

Emma hugged her best friend. "That would be great. I know how much you miss your daughter." Lisa, her daughter by her first marriage, had died at five.

"You know how scared I was when I was pregnant with Nicholas. Maybe I shouldn't risk having another."

Emma held up her hand. "Shh. You aren't to think like that. Turn this over to God and don't worry. It doesn't do you any good."

"I know." Abbey sighed. "Let's talk about you for a while. What are you preparing for Jake tonight?"

Emma shrugged. "I don't know. He was no help at all. What if I fix something he doesn't like?"

Laughing, Abbey shook her forefinger. "No. No. Didn't you just tell me not to worry?"

Emma's cheeks burned. "I didn't say I always follow my own advice."

"You cook what you and Josh will enjoy. I have a feeling Jake will like it, too. If not, he had his chance to get what he wanted. What I really want to know is did you say anything to Josh last night about Carson and Sean?"

Emma lowered her gaze. Yesterday she'd rehearsed with Abbey how she was going to tell Josh. "No. The right time didn't present itself."

"You chickened out."

"No, he came home from school in a bad mood. I didn't want to make it worse."

"Shh. Here come Josh and Madi. You better say something before this evening." Abbey lowered her voice. "Isn't the point of the dinner with Jake—to have him help Josh? That won't happen if Josh doesn't know what's going on."

"I know."

It was one reason for seeing Jake again. But equally important, she wanted Jake to work with Shep. There was something about the man that caused her to think of him at odd moments throughout the day. Last night she had even dreamed about him. They were in the park throwing a ball for Shep to fetch. Then she remembered why she'd awakened suddenly. Her son had been there grinning, happy. The scene gave her a feeling of family. She mentally shook herself. She would help Jake, but she wasn't looking for anything beyond friendship.

"Are you ready to go? I'm supposed to be at Craig's in half an hour," Josh said, stopping in front of her.

"Yes, I have to go to the grocery store and then start dinner."

"Do I hafta go tonight? I'm sure I could stay with Craig."

"I'd hoped you'd help me convince Mr. Tanner to take Shep."

"Okay. I guess I can since he helped me last Saturday." Josh headed inside with Madi, the two talking about the new terrier.

"Smooth. He has no idea what you're really doing," Abbey whispered close to Emma's ear.

"Hush," Emma said, then louder she called out to the little girl, "Hey, Madi. What's the terrier's name? I'll start training her next week."

Abbey's sister-in-law turned around. "Buttons. Josh and me decided that today."

"See you all tomorrow at church." Emma followed her son out to her gray PT Cruiser. If she was going to say anything to him, she had to now while she could focus on the conversation rather than driving. Inside her car, she shifted to face Josh in the front passenger seat. "I've discovered the names of two of the boys who attacked you last weekend."

He grew rigid. "Who?"

"Carson O'Neil and Sean Phillips. It's only a matter of time before I find out who the third guy is. You might as well tell me."

His blue eyes became big and round, fear inching into them. "No. I can't. And you can't say anything to anyone about Carson and Sean. Promise me, Mom."

"They really have you scared. How? Why?"

"Because they're mean."

"Carson? He used to be a friend of yours."

"Well, he's not anymore. He thinks Sean and…" His eyes bored into her. "Oh, never mind. You don't care about me. If you say anything to their parents or them, it'll only get worse for me. Is that what you want?"

Conflicting emotions crammed her throat, making it impossible to reply. Her stomach roiled with frustration and her own fear she wouldn't be able to help her son with this problem. But Josh's anguish pierced her. She felt so inadequate to make everything all right for him. He and his father had had such a close relationship. Sam would have known the right thing to do in this situation.

She straightened behind the steering wheel and started the engine. "I'm friends with Carson's mother. I'll start there, and if there's any backlash, I want to know about it." As she pulled away from Caring Canines, she glanced at Josh.

Turned away from her, he stared out the side window, his left hand opening and closing.

"Josh?"

"Sure. Why don't you follow me around? That

oughta work and alert everyone in school my mother fights my battles."

"If I could to protect you, I would. I know you have to learn to deal with these boys, but you may need help."

With his back still to her, he ran his hands through his brown hair. "How did ya find out their names?"

"I have my resources."

"Which friend snitched?"

She didn't want to tell him Jake identified the two in the yearbook, but she didn't want her child angry at his friends. He needed them. For a few seconds, she thought of lying, but that never worked and would only make the situation worse. "Mr. Tanner."

Josh twisted around. "How? He didn't know their names."

"I brought him your yearbook, and he found them in it."

Silence reigned the rest of the way to Craig's house, and the frosty atmosphere underscored how mad her son was. The second she stopped, Josh thrust open the door and hurried toward his friend's place.

"I'll pick you up at six-twenty," Emma yelled. She would call Craig's mother and let her know.

Now more than ever she needed Jake to help her son cope with the bullying. If her son would even talk to him.

Saturday night, carrying a cardboard box full of the food for dinner, Emma approached Jake's house with her son shuffling his feet at least three yards behind her. She set the meal down on the porch and waited for Josh who led Shep on a leash. Other than telling her again he didn't want to come to Mr. Tanner's, he said nothing in the car when she picked him up at Craig's.

"I expect you to use appropriate behavior tonight."

Josh's bottom lip stuck out farther. "It's none of his business."

"The minute he stepped in and helped you it became his business. It's like a person witnessing a crime. He has an obligation to come forward and report it. That's the right thing to do. And beating up someone, especially three to one is wrong. If adults do that to one another, they are charged with a crime and jailed."

"Can't you trust me to handle my own problems? I don't butt in with yours."

"Guess what? I'm your mom and that's part of my duty as a parent." She rang the doorbell then scooped up the box. She was beginning to think it was a bad idea including Josh, but she wanted Jake to help her son.

When Jake let them inside, Emma fixed a bright smile on her face, determined to go ahead with her plans, even if her son wasn't cooperating. In the past Josh rarely held a grudge long, but lately he'd changed so she had no idea how he would act with Jake.

"It's nice to see you again, Josh," Jake said as he closed the front door, his back to them.

Which was a good thing because her son scowled. Emma clasped his shoulder and squeezed gently. Josh's expression morphed into a neutral one.

Jake swung around. "I've been anticipating a home-cooked meal all day."

Emma smiled, hoping it would cover the fact her child wasn't being too friendly. "I'm going to put this enchilada casserole in your oven to reheat. Josh, why don't you show Mr. Tanner some of the things Shep does in the backyard?"

Displeased by that suggestion, her son huffed and headed to the back door with Shep in tow.

As Emma put the salad bowl in the refrigerator, Jake moved to her and waited until the back door clicked closed. "He knows I pointed out the boys in the yearbook?"

Emma nodded, her throat thick.

"Did something happen between Josh and them?"

She faced him, just a few inches of space between them. Her heartbeat kicked up a notch. "No, not that I know of. I haven't done anything about the two boys yet. I'm going to talk to Carson's mother tomorrow. I thought I would see her after church. Find out what she thinks, especially about Sean. I wanted Josh to know before I did it."

"And he wanted to know how you found out?" No emotions indicated what Jake was feeling.

"Yes, I'm sorry. I didn't want him to know, but I can't lie to my son. If you want us to go home, I'll leave the food and we'll take off."

"No. You went to a lot of trouble to cook a meal for us. Besides, it's time I have a talk with your son if you still want me to. Avoiding this won't solve any problems, either."

"You don't mind?" She inhaled a deep breath, laced with his lime aftershave.

"Your son needs help. The second I decided to break up the fight I made that decision. Bullies shouldn't be tolerated. If something isn't done now, it'll only get worse." He started for the back door.

"Jake," she said. When he glanced at her, she continued, "I didn't think you wanted to get involved. What changed your mind?"

His gaze was riveted to hers. Intense. Compelling. "You."

There was so much feeling behind that one word. She attempted a laugh that came out shaky. "You mean I wore you down?"

"Not exactly. But the compassion you've shown me, even when I tried to reject it, reminded me how beneficial it is to help others. Maybe then I won't think about my own problems all the time."

She grinned. "So you're taking Shep?"

"Maybe. If we're a good fit. I've been reading up on service dogs, and I talked with Ben this afternoon."

"You did? I didn't think you would call him."

"Can't a guy change his mind?"

"Sure." She shooed him outside. "Then go see Shep."

His chuckles lingered in the air as he left. The sound warmed her. She closed her eyes for a moment, immediately picturing the laugh lines at the corners of his eyes deepening and the edges of his mouth tilting up. The image sent goose bumps spreading over her. She rubbed her hands up and down her arms as though she could erase his effect on her.

In his backyard Jake slowly eased himself down on the step next to Josh. The boy stiffened but didn't move away. Instead, he lobbed a tennis ball for Shep to retrieve.

"Does he like to do that a lot?" Jake asked, not sure how to approach an angry eleven-year-old to deal with a problem he probably thought was unsolvable. He could remember feeling that way on more than one occasion.

For a long moment Josh's mouth remained clamped. "Yeah," he said finally.

"That's good to know."

When Shep trotted back to Josh, he dropped the ball in the child's lap, then sat waiting. Jake petted the German shepherd while the dog's attention was on the boy's hand. Josh didn't toss the ball but instead squeezed it over and over.

"I know you aren't happy that your mom wants to talk with Carson's mother or that I pointed out the two boys in the yearbook to her," Jake said, hoping to get a reaction out of Josh and a chance to approach the subject of bullying.

A frown descended on Josh's face, the quiet lengthening. Jake searched for another way to start a conversation. He'd led men into battle, but this wasn't an area of expertise for him. About the only qualification he had for this was that he had been a boy once.

"Why did you show her their pictures? I thought you weren't going to tell her." Disappointment leaked into Josh's voice and expression.

And that bothered Jake more than the child's anger. "I told you that I wouldn't say anything about the fight because you were going to. Some things you can't hide from a mother, and being beaten up like you were is one of them. What did you expect her to do? Not to care and let it keep happening? Do you think that's realistic, knowing your mother?"

Josh shook his head. "I was going to hide from her until I looked better."

"That would be days, possibly a couple of weeks. Do you think that would have worked?"

"She's doing exactly what I knew she would: interfering."

"Because she's acting like a typical mother. You should have seen my mom when I was first beaten up by some bullies."

Josh twisted around and pressed his back against the wooden railing on the stairs and the decking, his focus on Jake's arms. His muscles were evident since he was wearing a short-sleeved shirt. "You were bullied? You're *huge*."

"I was small when I was your age." The subject still bothered Jake. He'd been taught by his father never to show weakness. As stress began to blanket him, he continued to stroke Shep. "It seemed like everyone was bigger than I was. In sixth grade one boy was determined to make my life miserable. When my mother found out and told my dad, he went to the other guy's parents."

Hope brightened Josh's blue eyes. "He left you alone after that?"

"No, he didn't. His dad even looked the other way. Later I found out that his dad behaved that way and didn't see anything wrong with it. He got his way by intimidating others."

The boy's shoulders slumped. "So you kept having trouble."

"Yes, I kept having trouble, but my attitude began changing. I was determined not to be a victim. I started exercising and making myself as strong and capable as I could. I was small at that time, but that didn't mean I couldn't use my wits. I found out other kids were being bullied by these boys, too. We stuck together and helped each other. A lot can happen when you realize you aren't alone."

Josh moved down a step closer to Shep and hugged the dog. "I told the lady who supervises recess at lunch about Sean and the other guys last week. They got me alone at the side of the building and took my money then pushed me down in the mud. She didn't do anything."

"Why not?"

"She didn't see it. They said I was lying, but I had mud all over my clothes. That's why they beat me up in the park the next day. To teach me a lesson." Josh rubbed his face against Shep's neck, and some of the tension dissolved from his features.

Watching the interaction between the dog and the boy reinforced what Jake had heard and read about service dogs for people with PTSD. "If one person at school doesn't do anything about it, go to another. Find someone who'll listen to you. From what your mother's told me, your teacher seems sympathetic. Start with her."

"But they'll come after me."

"Possibly. I can teach you a few self-defense moves when you're cornered, but try to outsmart them. Don't put yourself in a place where they can get you alone. Have friends around you. If you see them, get to a safe place where others are."

"But they'll call me a chicken."

"For defending yourself any way you can? I call that smart. Even the United States Armed Forces use defensive moves to protect themselves."

Josh straightened on the step, his shoulders back. "Yeah." Shep barked a couple of times, nudging Josh's hand with the ball. "Do you want to throw it for him?"

"Sure." Jake took the ball and hurled it so far it ended up at the back of the fence on the one-acre piece of property.

"Wow!" Eyes wide, Josh looked at him. "Did ya play baseball or something?"

"In college I was on the baseball team."

"Where?"

"Oklahoma University. I got my degree in psychology."

"I want to go there. My dad did."

When Shep returned, he released the ball at Jake's feet. Jake snatched it up and gave it to Josh. "Your turn."

"I can't do what you did."

"I wouldn't expect you to. I played the sport for years and practiced a lot. I also lift weights to keep my muscles in my arms strong."

"When did you start playing?"

"When I was ten. Are you on a team?"

"I thought about it last spring, but I didn't try out. I'm not very good. Maybe next spring if I can get better."

"When you throw the ball, put your whole body into it, not just the arm you're using."

Josh rose and tried to do what Jake had said. The ball flew a couple of yards farther.

"That's better. With practice you'll improve. It's a good way to build up your body." Jake heard the screen door open and close behind him. The hairs on his nape tingled as if Emma were staring at him. "If you want, we can practice a couple of times a week. I'll also teach you those defensive techniques." He looked behind him. "That is, if it's okay with your mom."

Josh whirled around. "Is it? Did ya see him throw the ball? He's *good.*"

"If Mr. Tanner doesn't mind, that's fine with me." Emma's eyes glinted with a smile—aimed at Jake.

"I don't. We can use my backyard. It's big enough even to work on batting, at least at the beginning. But we'll need a fielder since I'm not ready to do too much running after the ball." Jake turned his attention to Emma, who was wearing a look that had power to slice through the barriers he'd erected. "Do you know anyone who can do that?"

Pink tinted her cheeks. She lowered her eyelids, veiling her expression. "If you can be patient, I will. I got hit with a baseball when I was a kid and can't say that I'm very good at putting myself in the way of one. My first instinct is to run from it."

Laughter welled up in Jake, and its release felt good. Even better, Josh and Emma joined in.

"Josh, you need to go wash your hands. Then please get the salad and dressing out of the refrigerator and set the table with the paper goods I brought."

When the boy disappeared inside, Jake used the wooden railing to hoist himself to his feet and faced Emma at the top of the steps. "We had a good conversation. He wasn't very happy with me at first, but he listened to my explanation."

"I'm so glad you volunteered to help. You should see me throwing a ball. Not a pretty picture. I have never been athletic. Actually, as you heard, I'm pretty much a wimp."

"A cute one."

Her blush deepened. She looked down for a few seconds before lifting her head. "Are you sure you want to do this? I know a lot is going on in your life and I don't want to add—"

"Stop right there. I wouldn't have offered if I didn't mean it. Josh reminds me of when I was young. When I struggled with bullies, I had a father to help me. Josh doesn't." When Shep planted himself next to him, he stroked the dog's head as though he'd been doing it for a long time.

"How are you and Shep getting along?"

"Fine."

"He can stay the night if you like."

"You're one determined lady. I don't have anything for a dog."

"I've fed him already today. I could come pick him up tomorrow morning before going to church. It would give you a chance to bond with him without doing the day-to-day care. Then if you want to try longer, I can help you get what you need and show you how to work with Shep."

"Ben warned me about you. You did the same thing to him." Jake mounted the steps. "You do know that Josh is attached to Shep?"

"Yes. He's that way with every dog I bring home to train."

"He needs his own dog. I saw that earlier when we were talking about being bullied."

"He talked to you about that?"

"Yes, after I told him what happened to me. Maybe Shep should stay with you and Josh."

"No, I'm bringing home a new dog that would fit Josh better. I've seen him with Buttons at Caring Canines. She responds with him already. I could involve him in Buttons's training."

Leaning on his cane, Jake opened the back door, and Emma went inside ahead of him. The aroma from the dinner reheating filled his kitchen and enticed his taste buds. He hadn't been eating as well as he should, but this evening he planned on having a second helping, and he hadn't tasted the dish yet. But anything that smelled this good had to be delicious.

"Take a seat, guys. I'll get the casserole out of the oven, and then we're ready to eat."

Both Josh and Jake washed their hands, then Josh sat while Jake remained standing and waited until Emma had placed the casserole on a trivet in the center of the table. He pulled out a chair for her. She flashed him a surprised look but eased down onto it. Then he took his seat.

"Do you mind if we pray?" Emma asked, reaching across the table to take Josh's hand, then offering hers to Jake.

He clasped it, and the feel of her small one surrounded by his larger grasp seemed so right to him. Astounded by that sensation, he almost released it.

But Emma bowed her head and said a prayer over the food, concluding with, "Please, Lord, put a wall of protection around Josh and Jake. Amen." She squeezed his hand then let it go.

Stunned, Jake couldn't think of anything to say. To be included in the prayer with her son spoke of her depth of caring. The gesture touched his heart as nothing else had in months. Somehow he would return her kindness by aiding Josh with his problem.

Chapter Five

Later, in Jake's living room, Emma sat on one end of the couch while Josh curled up at the other and fell asleep. After dinner he had asked Jake to show him a self-defense move, and they had practiced while Emma and Shep watched. Jake demonstrated how Josh could use his arms to form a triangle to block certain punches. Josh had wanted to go over the move again and again until finally Emma called a halt.

Fatigue lined Jake's face, and yet he stayed right there trying to help her son. She didn't like the idea of Josh fighting, but she understood he needed to defend himself, especially when she remembered her child's injuries. The cuts and bruises were healing, but Josh's self-esteem was damaged.

"Thank you for working with Josh. I hope he never has to use any of those moves, but at least he knows them." Emma had wanted to smooth the tired lines from Jake's face, but instead she curled her hands at her sides.

"He'll need to practice them until they become second nature."

She winced. "He's eleven. This isn't something he should have to know."

"Like you, I hope he doesn't have to use them. I know how to snap a man's neck and kill him, but that doesn't mean I ever want to use that skill. If someone were trying to kill me, though, I'd protect myself. Those boys could have done a lot worse damage to Josh. They could have injured his eye, broken his nose, caused a concussion just to name a few things."

Emma's stomach knotted. "I get it. You don't have to convince me. But isn't there a peaceful way to take care of this problem?" Was that too much to ask a warrior?

"When people decide they aren't going to tolerate bullying, then yes. When others stand up and say no, that makes a difference. No tolerance is the best policy, but it takes a majority of people pitching in to make that work."

"Maybe I can get other mothers to help fight the bullying."

"There are probably organizations out there. Check and see what they're doing."

"I will. I'll do an internet search when I get

home." She rose and stretched her stiff muscles. It had been a long, tiring week. "So what have you decided about keeping Shep overnight?"

Shep lay at Jake's feet. The dog's ears perked forward, and he sat up. Jake patted Shep then ran his fingers through the German shepherd's fur. "I'd like to give it a try." Standing, he gripped his cane. "Where does he usually sleep?"

"In his crate. I didn't want him to get too used to sleeping somewhere special in my house since he wouldn't be there long."

"Should I have the crate, then?"

"Try without it. You can fix up a bed with a blanket on the floor. I'd suggest in your bedroom. That'll strengthen your bond. If there's a problem, give me a call—anytime."

As they talked, Emma realized they kept stepping closer to each other. To her surprise, she wanted to touch him, reassure him this would work. Still, she kept her arms by her sides. "Okay?"

"I can't ask Josh to help himself if I won't at least give this a try. He's a smart kid. He'll figure that out. I'll be fine."

"I know you will. Shep's a good service dog. When I've had a particularly bad day, he's sensed that and is right next to me, rubbing against my leg or nudging my hand to pet him."

"That's a good reason for Josh to have one. As

I said before, I don't want to take anything away from your son."

Without thinking, she started to place two fingers against his lips but stopped herself inches away from him. "Not another word." The feel of his breath against her fingertips tickled, and she dropped her arm back to her side. "I'll involve Josh in the new dog's training, and if Josh wants to keep her, we will."

Jake's eyes shone as they roamed over her facial features. "You have your hands full working two jobs. Do you have to work so hard?"

"I'm still paying off my husband's medical bills. The hospital is patient, but I want the debt paid off this year. Then I might be able to cut my hours at Harris Animal Hospital and devote more time to training. The demand for service and therapy dogs is growing."

He lifted his hands but dropped them back to his sides, a hesitance entering his expression. "It sounds like you need to relax."

She attempted a smile. "I watched my parents struggle with debt, and it nearly destroyed their marriage. I worked hard never to have any until Sam went into the hospital. Then it was like the floor fell from beneath me. My life changed in an instant."

He stepped back. "I know that feeling firsthand."

"I know there are no guarantees in life, but it

seems I take one step forward, then two back."
In his eyes she saw a reflection of her concerns.
He was going through the same thing for different reasons. In that moment she experienced a kinship with him she hadn't felt with anyone but her husband. The realization left her speechless.

Sounds of her son waking up propelled her back a few paces. When she turned toward him on the couch, he opened his eyes slowly and looked from her to Jake.

"What did I miss?" Sleepiness coated his words.

"Not much, kiddo," said Jake. "I've agreed to take Shep tonight and see how it works."

For a fleeting moment, a frown skittered across Josh's face.

"This way we can concentrate on making Buttons feel at home her first night at our house," Emma said, glad to see Josh looking more relaxed. "I was thinking of letting her stay in your room at night if you think that's okay."

He perked up and scooted to a sitting position. "Sure. She'll probably be lonely without the other dogs at Caring Canines."

"That's what I was thinking."

Josh rubbed his eyes then peered at Jake. "Can I come visit Shep sometime?"

"Yes. Don't forget we'll be working on your baseball skills and self-defense. There'll be plenty of time for you to see Shep."

The boy grinned. "Yeah, right." He hopped to his feet, started for the foyer but paused a moment to pat Shep and say goodbye, then continued his trek toward the front door.

Emma laughed. "I guess we're leaving." She turned to follow Josh. "Call if you need me."

"Okay." He waited until Josh went onto the porch, then lowered his voice. "I hope your conversation with Carson's mother goes well tomorrow."

For a short time tonight she'd forgotten what she needed to do. She prayed Sandy would be receptive. It wasn't a conversation she was looking forward to. "Can I ask you a favor?"

One of his eyebrows rose. "Yes, you can ask, but I won't guarantee I'll do it." One side of his mouth turned up.

"I have an idea. I'd like to drop Josh off at two then go see Sandy at her house where it's more private. I don't think it'll take long. But if you'd rather not watch Josh, just say so. I'll understand."

Jake glanced over her shoulder at the boy. "No problem. We can practice the moves he learned today."

The urge to hug Jake swamped her. Instead, she murmured, "Thanks," then scratched Shep behind his ears and left. Josh knelt next to Shep and rubbed his hand down the length of his back. "Goodbye, boy."

As her son descended the porch steps, he said, "You know, Mr. Tanner isn't so bad. I'm not mad at him anymore for showing you those guys' pictures. I've been thinking. If Dad had been alive, I'd probably have told him who they were. He'd have understood."

"And you don't think I would?"

"You're a girl. Girls freak out about fighting."

She stopped on the sidewalk, blocking her son's path. "I don't condone fighting, but I want you to be able to protect yourself long enough to get away."

"Sure, Mom."

"Self-defense is one thing. Being aggressive is totally different. Understood?"

"Yeah. I'd be stupid to pick a fight with them. They're bigger than me, except for Carson."

"I'm glad we understand each other." She draped her arm over his shoulder and began walking.

Jake sat in his bedroom that night staring at Shep, who was sitting on his makeshift bed. The German shepherd had scratched and walked around in circles then finally settled onto the two blankets.

"I'm not sure how this is going to work, but if you're willing to give this a chance, I am, too."

Shep cocked his head, his ears sticking up.

"I still don't see how you can really help. I hope you prove me wrong."

Jake switched off his light and lay on his bed, tired from lack of sleep and overextending himself with Josh. Still, he felt as if he had made a difference. For a long time he kept his eyes open and stared up, the digital clock on his radio throwing shadows on the ceiling. But slowly his eyelids grew heavy and slid closed, whisking him into a world of dreams he would avoid if he could....

The noise of gunfire cracked the air around him. Boom, boom rocked the ground beneath him. He lunged for shelter, screaming to his men to do likewise.

Something wet and rough scraped across his cheek, followed by a loud sound. Barking? Jake's eyes popped open to find Shep propped up on his hind legs against Jake's bed. The dog's tongue swept him again. Jake fumbled for the light and turned it on. Shep nosed Jake's nearest hand, and he began petting the dog.

Had he screamed out loud? Awakened the dog? Or had Shep sensed something wasn't right? Either way, Shep had managed to stop his nightmare before it became full-fledged. That the German shepherd could do exactly what Emma had described amazed Jake. He scooted over and patted the top of his coverlet. Shep jumped up on the bed and stretched out beside Jake.

With the light off again and one hand on the dog, Jake went to sleep, feeling hope for the first time in months.

On Sunday afternoon Sandy O'Neil gestured toward a wingback in her living room. "Have a seat, Emma. You sounded serious at church today. Is something wrong?"

Emma's heartbeat tapped out a fast tempo against her rib cage. All the way to Sandy's house she'd practiced what she would say to her friend, and every word she'd come up with fled her mind.

"Emma?"

She swallowed then said, "Last weekend Josh was jumped by three boys in the park. As you could see today, he has bruises, a cut on his lip and above his eye."

"I wondered about that, but I figured if you wanted to tell me about it you'd say something. I asked Carson on the ride home if he knew what happened. He told me Josh was in a fight."

"Yes, one that was completely lopsided and not of his choosing."

"I'm sorry to hear that."

Emma gripped her hands, rubbing her thumb into her palm. "Thankfully, a man who lived near the park saw what was happening and broke it up before Josh was hurt worse. Two of the boys were bigger than my son. I know one was older. I'm not sure about the third kid."

Sandy covered her mouth with her fingers. "Oh, no. Do you know who did it?"

"Two of the boys and I thought Carson could help me with the third one."

"Josh doesn't know who he is?"

"Yes, but he's scared to say anything."

Sandy pushed to her feet. "Carson's out back. I'll call him in and see if he and Josh talked. They aren't in the same class this year so they might not have."

"Wait before you ask Carson to join us. The reason I know Carson can tell me the name of the third boy is because your son was one of the three beating up Josh."

Sandy collapsed onto the couch across from Emma, the color washing from her face. "Not Carson. He doesn't know how to fight. Josh told you he did?"

"No, but I asked Jake Tanner, the man who stopped it, to look at the yearbook from last spring and see if he could find any of the boys. He picked out Carson and Sean Phillips. Then I talked to Josh, and he admitted it. My son is afraid of retaliation, so he didn't want me to know who's bullying him."

Sandy cringed. "My son? A bully? I don't see that. I didn't raise him like that."

"I know. That's why I'm here talking to you. Carson and Josh were friends once. I know they drifted apart but…" Emma's throat jammed with helplessness and frustration.

"They had a falling-out, and Carson would never say why."

"Neither would Josh."

"I'll be right back. We need to get to the bottom of this." Sandy shot to her feet and marched toward the back of the house.

Emma took a deep breath, then another, but her lungs still didn't feel as if they had enough oxygen. The whole affair left her sick to her stomach. She heard Sandy call Carson inside, and the boy stomped toward the living room, denying he did anything wrong.

Lord, please guide me with what to do. Let the truth come out.

When Carson entered, he saw Emma and immediately lowered his head and pinched his lips together.

"Hi, Carson. I haven't seen you much but occasionally at church. I've missed you coming over to the house."

Sandy nudged her child farther into the room. "Sit. We need to talk to you." While her son obeyed, she continued, "Did you take part in beating up Josh last weekend in the park?"

Seconds ticked away without an answer, then

finally Carson raised his head, tears in his eyes. "Yes. But I had to."

"Why?" His mother sat next to him.

"If I didn't, they'd have done it to me. I was scared." Carson's lower lip quivered.

Emma's heart cracked at the sight of Carson's fear—much like Josh's when he wasn't trying to mask it. "Who are they? Sean Phillips. Who else?"

Carson blinked rapidly. "Josh told you about Sean?"

"No. The man who caught you fighting identified Sean and you. Who's the third boy?"

"If he thought I said anything, I'd…" His voice faded, replaced with crying, tears running down Carson's face.

Emma looked at Sandy. Her face reflected shock that slowly transformed into anger. Emma sat back in her chair, forcing her tight muscles to relax. She needed to let Sandy deal with Carson. She knew her friend would do the right thing.

Sandy wound her arms around her son and brought him against her while he sobbed. "Emma, we'll talk, and I'll call you later with the third boy's name. Then all four of us need to talk. This can't continue."

"I agree. Bullies in our neighborhood and school can't be tolerated." Emma rose. "I can see myself out. Thank you, Sandy. Goodbye, Carson."

"I should be thanking you for bringing this problem to my attention."

Emma left the O'Neils' house. Hope seeded in her heart, and she prayed it would grow. That they would come up with a solution to help their sons and others.

Emma drove to Jake's place in ten minutes and parked in the driveway. Josh had wanted to bring Buttons over to see Jake and Shep, but she'd told him maybe some other time. When she'd gone in to wake her son for church, Buttons had been sleeping right next to Josh, his arms lying over the terrier. This was one animal she decided she wouldn't train for Caring Canines, and she knew Abbey would understand, especially with what was going on in her son's life right now.

The sounds of her son and Jake talking came from the backyard. She headed for the gate and let herself in. When she rounded the corner of the house, Josh hurled a baseball the farthest she had ever seen and Shep ran to fetch it.

Emma approached Josh and Jake by the deck. "I don't think you're going to need me to be a fielder. Shep's doing a great job."

"He loves to get the ball, Mom. I'll teach Buttons to do the same thing."

"So I can leave and come back when you're through?"

Jake shook his head and smiled. "You can be the cheerleader."

For the next half hour Jake patiently worked with her son to show him the correct way of throwing a baseball. As she cheered on Josh, she watched Jake and saw the traits of a good leader—he provided honesty when Josh needed instruction, support even when he didn't quite get the move right, confidence as they practiced again and again.

When Jake sat on the deck steps, Josh plopped down next to him, breathing hard from his exertion. Shep joined the pair and lay down on the grass nearby.

"I'm changing hats. I'm going to be the water girl. You all look like you could use some."

Jake leaned back, bracing himself with his elbows. "Sounds good. How about you, Josh?"

Her son followed suit, relaxing against the stair behind him. "Yep, with lots of ice."

Emma mounted the steps between the two and went inside the kitchen. After serving and cleaning up the night before, she was familiar with Jake's setup and in no time found the glasses and a bowl for Shep. She filled a pitcher with ice and water, put everything on a tray, then returned to the deck.

"How did the self-defense lesson go?" After

passing the drinks to everyone, including the dog, she sat down behind her son at the top of the stairs.

Jake slid her a glance. "Good, but it's not easy to practice with Josh when I'm so much taller. Maybe I can show you a few moves, and you two can go through them. It wouldn't hurt for you to know these in case you're ever attacked."

Josh's eyes grew round and his body tensed.

Emma hurriedly said to her son, "That's nothing for you to worry about. It never hurts to be prepared. Just as a precaution, hon."

"Mom's still a lot taller than me." Josh's stiff posture eased, and he gulped down most of the water in his glass.

"Jake, are you back here?" Marcella Kime came around the corner with a basket. She smiled. "I thought I heard you."

Out of the corner of his mouth, Jake murmured, "Sunday afternoon is always one of her days to bring some food to fatten me up. She thinks I've lost too much weight."

"I heard that, and I'm right." Marcella set the basket down on the step then bent over to pet Shep. "He's adorable. It's about time you got some companionship." His neighbor's gaze flitted from the dog to Emma. "Nice to see you here. Jake is way too introverted. That's my vocabulary word for today."

"What's it mean?" Josh peeked into the basket, licking his lips.

"You can have one, kiddo. She brings enough to feed an army. I'll let Miss Kime explain since it's her word."

"Introverted means someone who likes to be alone. Jake, all my goodies can be put in the freezer to enjoy another day. Dig in, Josh. It's my cookies with both white-and-milk chocolate chips and walnuts." Marcella lifted the basket for Emma's son.

"Mmm. Thanks, Miss Kime. This is great," Josh said with his mouth full.

"Josh." Emma gave him "the look" to remember his manners, then took a bite of a cookie, savoring its rich taste. "I hope I can get this recipe. These are delicious."

Marcella nodded. "I have all these great recipes and no children to pass them on to. Come by one day and you can take what you want and make a copy of it."

"Love to. I'll give you a call."

Marcella set her hand on her waist and peered at Jake. "What do you think?"

"Since I'm an introvert, I thought I should keep quiet." He grinned and popped the last bit of his cookie into his mouth and chewed it. "Perfect as always."

Marcella beamed. "Music to my ears. That's

why I bake. I love hearing how much people enjoy what I make." She started for the gate. "Share with your friends. I'll make you some more tomorrow." As she went around the side of the house, she waved.

Reaching for another cookie, Jake laughed. "I'm not sure there are going to be any left to share."

Josh looked from Jake to Emma. "I worked up an appetite. I should have asked Miss Kime to help me demonstrate my moves." He hopped up. "Maybe I should ask her—"

"No," both Emma and Jake said at the same time.

Emma looked at Jake who added, "She may be the right height, but if you accidentally broke one of her bones, you would feel awful."

"Older people have more brittle bones and aren't in as good shape as—"

Marcella popped her head around the corner of the house. "I heard that. I may be having trouble with the lock that keeps sticking on your gate, but I have strong bones and would love to help."

Josh stood to his full four feet ten inches. "I don't want to hurt you."

"You aren't going to hurt me. I'm in tip-top shape." The older woman strolled back to the group. "What have you learned?"

The boy swung his gaze to Emma then Jake, mouthing the words, *Help me.*

Jake pulled himself up and with his cane approached Marcella, gesturing for Josh to join them. "I showed him how to block some punches by forming a triangle with his arms. Since it's such a large discrepancy between my height and his, it's easier for him to practice with a person closer to his height."

The petite neighbor, still wearing her church clothes—a flowery dress, a hat and one-inch high heels—said, "I'm ready and willing. What do you want me to do?"

"Grab the front of his T-shirt near the collar." Jake demonstrated.

Marcella rubbed her palms together, her eyes gleaming. When she made her move toward Josh, his expression was wary. Marcella clutched the cotton by his neck and moved in closer. Leaning back, he brought his arms up as though to ward her off and crossed one over to clasp his forearm, then brought the locked move down on his "attacker."

"Good, Josh!" Jake said. "You broke the hold. Depending on the circumstances you can go for various vulnerable spots or hopefully, since you're already leaning back, you can turn and run. Get to a place where there are people."

Emma watched as Jake put Josh and Marcella through a couple of different scenarios using the triangle hold. Her son's attention stayed totally focused on Jake.

At the end, Marcella stroked her chin. "You know, I have some friends who would love to learn how to protect themselves. Me, for one. Then there is Bertha, Florence and—"

Jake's expression went blank. "I don't mind your participating when I work with Josh. You two are close in size. But I don't have time to do classes. I..." His voice sputtered to a halt. He pivoted and started for the deck stairs. "Thank you, Miss Kime, for helping us. I'm afraid all of this activity has tired me out."

"Remember, call me Marcella."

"Josh, go with Miss Kime and help her with the gate and make sure she gets home all right. I'll meet you out front by the car." Emma gestured toward the side yard.

Josh's forehead creased. "Okay." He watched Jake who was opening the back door, Shep on his heels. Josh went to Emma and whispered, "Is he okay?"

"Yes. You know how Uncle Ben would get when he was recovering from his injuries. He may have overdone it today. I'm going to check with him about Shep then I'll be out front."

As her son and Marcella left, Emma snatched up the pitcher with the three glasses and hurried after Jake before he closed the door and locked her out. Worry nibbled at her. The sight of him shutting down reminded her of Ben. She didn't give up on her brother; she wouldn't on Jake, either.

Chapter Six

Emma stepped through the entrance into the kitchen as Jake was swinging the door closed, stopping him in midmotion.

He frowned. "I'm really tired."

"I won't keep you but a few minutes. I wanted to put these in your dishwasher and check with you about Shep."

Jake glanced at the dog, noticing he'd followed him into the house. "I want to keep him. But would you do me a favor?"

"Sure, anything. Josh has really responded to what you're teaching him."

"So did Marcella—too much." The thought of going somewhere and teaching self-defense had sent a bolt of panic through him. It was one thing to help Josh with a few moves, but he didn't want to be responsible for instructing others—not when he'd been unable to save his men from walking into an ambush. Their deaths felt like a bombed building crushing him beneath the rubble.

Emma put the pitcher and glasses in the dishwasher, then faced Jake. "What do you need me to do?"

He dug his wallet out of his back jean pocket and gave her some money. "If you'll get me everything that Shep needs, I'd appreciate it. You know what he's used to. Any toys. Treats. Food."

"We'll go after we leave here. Do you need anything for his bedding?"

"No, that's been taken care of." He remembered waking up this morning with Shep stretched out inches from him on top of the cover. His fingers instinctively went to stroke the dog's fur, and he'd known in that instant he didn't want to return Shep. A calmness flowed through him as he petted the German shepherd. If there had been any doubt left, Shep's eyes, conveying instant affection for Jake, would have erased it. The dog had low crawled what space had been between them and placed his head on Jake's chest, forging a bond that went straight to his heart.

Emotions swelled in his throat, and he turned away from Emma. "I'm going to take a nap so if you'll leave the items on the porch, I'll get them later. Please lock the door as you leave. Thanks for your help." He limped down the hall toward the living room.

From the foyer Emma said, "Bye. Thanks for helping Josh." Then the sound of the front door closing echoed through the house.

Total quiet, finally. Today the level of noise had strained Jake's nerves, yet working with Josh had made him feel good about himself, as if even with the shape he was in, he could still help someone. When he felt tension begin to take hold of him, he put his hand on Shep and the stress melted away.

Then the sight of Emma when she returned from seeing Carson's mother lifted his spirits. Her bright smile and twinkling eyes reminded him of the sunrays peeking through a bank of storm clouds.

He stretched out on the long couch, and Shep lay down on the carpet near him within reach. "I wonder how Emma's meeting with Sandy O'Neil went. Maybe I'll call her later and find out," he said to the dog, who cocked his head as he listened. "She's a special lady. Too bad we met at this time in my life."

All the way home from work, Emma tried to think of a way to check on Jake. It had been two days since she'd seen him. She had been Shep's trainer, so she should see how he was doing with the dog. *Yeah, right.* That wasn't the main reason she wanted to see or at least talk to him. She cared. The last look he had given her before hobbling out of the kitchen was a resigned one, as though he had come to the conclusion he would fight panic attacks for the rest of his life, that he wouldn't be able to deal with change easily or crowds. But that wasn't the case. People worked their way through PTSD. It wasn't easy, but it could be done, especially if he had a support system—people who cared. He had isolated himself.

At home Emma paced her kitchen, holding her cell and deliberating between calling Jake and putting her phone in her pocket. Josh would be home soon from Craig's. She'd stayed longer than usual at work, and Craig's mother had picked both boys up at school and taken them back to her house to work on a project for science. She appreciated her network of friends and parishioners who would help her if she needed it.

Jake was alone. Did he even turn to the Lord for guidance and strength? She couldn't have made it through Sam's death without God.

Staring down at her cell, she recited Jake's phone number, surprised she could remember it. Usually she had trouble recalling one unless she used it a lot. She'd only called him twice in the ten days she'd known him. She started to punch in a nine when the doorbell rang.

Odd. Josh had a key and would let himself into the house. Maybe it was Jake. She had no reason to believe that, but she hurried toward the entry hall, peered out the peephole and frowned.

When she swung the front door open, concern surged to the forefront. "Sandy, what's wrong?"

Her friend's swollen eyes indicated she'd been crying and right behind her was Carson, sniffling. One of his eyes would be black-and-blue by tomorrow.

Emma stepped to the side to allow them in. "Let's go into the living room, and you can tell me what happened."

Sandy sank onto the couch with Carson right next to her, his head hanging down. "I had a long talk with Carson last night about what we discussed on Sunday and told him he needed to apologize to Josh today at school for what he did. I also told him I'd better never hear that he's done that to anyone again."

As Sandy talked, her son's shoulders slumped, his chin now resting on his chest.

"I appreciate that, Sandy. Carson, why are you hurt?" The thought set alarm bells off in her mind.

"Tell her what happened at school, Carson."

The child started crying.

Sandy's forehead pinched into a frown. "That isn't going to help. You should never have become involved with Sean Phillips and Liam Rogers." She looked at Emma. "That's the third boy and the leader. He moved here this summer and should be in sixth grade but was held back. He is in Josh's class." She stopped for a few seconds, drawing in a deep breath.

Emma used that pause to say to Carson in a gentle voice, "Tell me about today. I haven't seen Josh yet. He's at Craig's house and should be home soon. Please help me to understand what's going on."

Carson sniffed and lifted his tear-streaked face. "I found Josh at recess and told him I was sorry about what happened in the park. I didn't want to hurt him, but if I hadn't, they would have turned on me. Liam likes to pick on smaller guys. When he didn't with me, I couldn't believe he wanted to be friends. Then he started going after Josh. I tried to back off. Liam said I was either on his side or against him."

"How can one or two boys have so much power over you all?" Emma knew Sean was about four or five inches taller than Josh, but Craig, her son's best friend, was almost that much taller, too.

"It's not just Liam and Sean. There are two others, both sixth-graders. They've got lots of kids scared. It's getting bad. They said no one better rat on them. They saw me talking with Josh and heard I told him I was sorry. They didn't like that. They paid me a visit." He touched the area by his eye and winced. "This was my warning."

"This has got to stop for your son and mine,"

Sandy said, twisting her hands together. She shook her head. "But I don't know what we can do. I'll talk with his teacher as well as the principal tomorrow about Liam."

Fear gripped Carson's face. "No, don't, Mom. *Please.*"

"That's what Josh kept telling me. But we can't stand by and let boys like Liam get away with what they're doing."

The sound of the front door being unlocked then opened announced Josh's arrival. Emma wasn't sure if she was glad for his timing or not. She wished Jake were here to help her with the situation. He might have some more insight that would aid them.

When Josh came into the living room, he stopped a few feet inside and stared at Carson. Her son's face went pale. "What happened?"

"Liam," Carson mumbled, and lowered his head again.

Thunder darkened her son's expression. "We need to take our school back."

Emma's mouth dropped open. His fierce tone shocked her. "What do you have in mind?"

"We've got to stand up to Liam and his buddies."

Carson shot a look at Josh. "How? They're bigger."

"I have a friend that's teaching me how to defend myself. Mom, do you think Mr. Tanner would help Carson and Craig? I talked to Craig about it."

"Honey, I don't know." *Especially after his reaction to Marcella's request.*

"Can you ask him?" Sandy inquired, all three of them staring at Emma.

She gulped. "I will."

After Carson and Sandy left, Josh turned to his mom. "Do you think Mr. Tanner will help us?"

"I don't know. Do you want to fight the bullies physically?" She still felt bothered about having Josh learn moves, even self-defense ones.

"No, there are better ways to settle disagreements. Mr. Tanner told me that. But I like knowing I can take care of myself. I've got some homework to do, but let me know when you talk with Mr. Tanner."

Josh left and Emma paced. This wasn't something she could talk about over the phone with him, and yet it was better not to surprise Jake by just showing up. She withdrew her cell from her pocket and punched in his number. Still, it would be good for him to be involved and give him something to think about other than what had occurred in Afghanistan.

"Shep and I are doing fine," Jake said in a husky voice, as though he hadn't used it a lot in the past few days.

The sound of it made her shiver, and an image

of the man occupied every inch of her mind. His handsome features—

"Emma?"

She blinked away the vision of him and said, "I need to see you. Can I come over?"

"You don't need to worry about Shep. You trained him well, and you've shown me the signals he responds to. We're doing fine."

"Please."

Jake held the phone to his ear while massaging his temple with his free hand. "Fine, I'm not going anywhere."

"Thanks. I'll be there in ten minutes."

When Emma hung up, Jake stood in his kitchen listening to the dial tone for a moment before disconnecting. The urgency in her voice spoke to the protector in him—something he hadn't tapped into much since his days in Afghanistan. Yet part of him was broken and lay in fear of the slightest loud noise, anything unexpected, the press of people, especially strangers.

Something was wrong. That much was clear from the tone of Emma's voice. Six months ago, before his world blew up around him, he would have been charging over to her house to fix whatever had her so concerned. She was Ben's little sister with no immediate family nearby.

It was bad enough that she haunted his waking

hours. Often when he looked at Shep, he thought about the time she must have put in to train the German shepherd. But whatever she needed— what if he couldn't do it? He'd already turned down Marcella's perfectly reasonable request. He was just so scared to have people begin to rely on him. Half his men were killed or wounded that day in the mountains. He'd let them down. He hadn't been able to bring them all out alive.

When he sat at his table to finish the frozen dinner he had microwaved, Shep came over and positioned himself next to Jake, laying his head in Jake's lap. Jake took his last bite, then stroked the dog, inhaling deep breaths to keep the anxiety at bay.

I can't fix everything. I can't control everything. He said those sentences over and over to himself while he ran his fingers through Shep's fur. *But the Lord can. Then why aren't You? Haven't I suffered enough?*

When the doorbell rang five minutes later, he was still seated at the table, petting Shep. He wanted to ignore the summons to answer, but he also felt the draw to help Emma as she was trying to help him.

"C'mon, Shep. Let's see what she needs." Jake shoved back his chair and strode toward the foyer. The thought that he might actually be able to do some good lifted his spirits.

With his dog by his side, he opened the door, his heartbeat increasing at the sight of Emma—beautiful, caring and in need. That was evident in the tiny lines wrinkling her forehead, the absence of a sparkle in her blue eyes.

"Come in. Let's go into the living room." He limped across the entry hall.

"You aren't using your cane."

"My physical therapist wants me to go without it as much as possible." He eased onto the couch. "He said I was using it more than I should. He's probably right." At least he could do without the physical crutch. Now if only he could get his life in order.

"How often do you go see him?" Emma took a seat at the other end of the sofa.

"He comes here twice a week." He saw the lines deepen on her forehead. "I do go out occasionally."

"When? No, forget I asked that. It isn't any of my business. But Shep can help you leave the house more."

He didn't want to talk about his problems. He was tired of dwelling on what he couldn't do anymore without fear of a panic attack. "Is this what you came to talk to me about? It sounded urgent on the phone."

"You know I talked to Sandy on Sunday about Carson. She insisted that he apologize to Josh.

Carson did at school today and later Liam Rogers, the third bully, made it clear he wouldn't tolerate that with Carson and punched him a few times. He'll have a black eye like Josh did."

"In other words, they're coercing Carson to be one of their followers."

"Yes, or at least not be a friend to Josh."

"Why are they targeting Josh?"

"Liam Rogers is in Josh's class. He was held back this year. Josh has always been well liked. Maybe Liam resents that. That's just a conjecture, but whatever the reason, he wants to make my son's life miserable."

Rage at the situation simmered in Jake's gut. He worked to tamp it down. "And you want me to do what?"

"Josh hoped you would work with Carson and Craig, his best friend, teaching them some of the self-defense moves. He feels if they can protect themselves they won't be so fearful all the time. It'll give them some self-confidence. Right now even Carson feels like a victim."

Was that the way he felt about himself—that he was a victim? Jake's first urge was to say no, but then he looked into Emma's hopeful face and the denial wouldn't form. Instead, he said determinedly, "On two conditions: it'll be done here, and there should be a fourth boy. That way I can pair them off to practice. But no more than four."

Four might even be too many. He'd taught self-defense and fighting skills to men—not children.

"That's great. Josh has another good friend named Zach. I'll talk with his parents and him to see if they'll agree. When can we start?"

Emma was like a dog that smelled a buried bone and would keep digging until it found the prize. "I figured that would be your next question," he said with a laugh. "Thursday. We'll work an hour Saturday, Tuesday and Thursday. Weekdays right after school and Saturday in the morning at ten. Okay?"

"It is with me. I'll check with the other parents and get back to you. If it is, I'll be here on Thursday to introduce you to everyone involved and to help if you need it."

He knew what she was doing. Since this would be a new situation, she wasn't sure if he would have a panic attack. The fact he couldn't reassure her he wouldn't frustrated him. Just another example of what little control he really had in his life.

"I'll call you tomorrow evening." Instead of rising to leave, Emma shifted to face him squarely. "So how are you and Shep getting along? Do you have any questions about his training?"

"In other words, what has he done for me?"

"Yes. He's capable of a lot."

"Every night he wakes me up before I get too far into my recurring nightmare about the ambush.

During the day, he senses when I need to calm down. I haven't gone anywhere since he came to live with me. We'll find out how that is at the first of next week when I go back to my doctor."

"How has it been in the past?"

"Not easy, but necessary. I have the first appointment in the morning and that helps, but I battle anxiety. I'm determined to overcome it." Amazed that he had admitted his fear to Emma, he realized in a short time he'd come to trust her. That surprised him even more.

"You should practice with short trips to different places. Shep will be able to help you with your anxiety before it really gets started."

"Can he stop panic attacks?"

"Possibly. It depends on what triggers an attack and how fast it comes on. I've got a proposition for you."

He tensed, not sure he wanted to hear it.

"You came to my house when you brought Josh home that first day. I could tell that was hard for you. What if you and Shep came to dinner tomorrow night? Since I'm just around the corner, it'd be a short trip."

"Then what?"

"Maybe the park or the ranch where I can show you the facilities for Caring Canines and then after that a store."

"All by Monday?"

"We can if you want, or do some after Monday."

Listening to her plan to help him with his panic attacks with crowds and unexpected situations, he felt anger mushroom inside him. He was an invalid and that didn't sit well. He swallowed what pride he had left and said, "Ben mentioned that your friend Abbey is a counselor and has a group for people who suffer with PTSD."

"Yes. No one in it is a veteran, so it might not be the right one for you. From what I understand, the vets in this area have to go to Oklahoma City for a PTSD therapy group. Abbey only started it a few months ago."

"Oklahoma City is two hours away."

"I know. Abbey's good. Try her group. The cause of the PTSD may be different from the others', but you all are still going through the same problems. I was glad Ben was in Tulsa where he had one for vets nearby. He never regretted attending."

Jake scrubbed his hands down his face, feeling the stubble of his beard. He'd forgotten to shave again this morning. "Do you know when the group meets?"

"Monday evenings. She has an office and room she uses at the ranch. She used to work at the hospital, but with the foundation growing, she quit that job to run Caring Canines. Still, she didn't want to give up some of the groups she'd started at the hospital. I'll give you her number. Let her know you're interested." Emma dug into her purse and withdrew a card. "Here's her number."

He took it from her, the brief brush of their fingers like an instant connection leaping between them. He didn't know if he could go to a therapy group and discuss his problems, but he had to do something. He didn't like what was happening, and it wasn't getting better with time. He needed more.

"I'll call her tomorrow, but with the doctor appointment on Monday, I'd rather push it to next week. I can start the group session the following Monday."

She smiled, those blue eyes light like the sea. "I hope you like pizza."

"Sure, but I can order that and bring it."

"No, this is homemade pizza. Josh and I usually have it on Wednesday night." She rose. "I'd better get back. I don't like to leave Josh too long by himself, even though he complains he's eleven. He thinks I baby him."

"You've been here awhile."

"I know but I'm only a block away and Buttons is becoming quite the watch dog. Not to mention I have a great neighbor."

The other day with Marcella, his neighbor, still bothered him. "I let Marcella down, but I'm not ready to do what she asked."

"What if this group with the four boys works out? Maybe then you can consider having the ladies over to your house. You could start with a small group and see what happens."

"I don't know. I don't want to commit to too much." He didn't want to let down any more people than he already had.

Jake walked Emma to the door and said goodnight. When she left, he felt lonely. She brought an energy into his house that teased him with future possibilities—that he could have a normal life again.

"You could open a pizzeria. That was delicious." Jake sat next to Emma on her porch swing the next evening, darkness blanketing the landscape beyond the security light by the front door. Shep lay stretched out nearby with his eyes trained on Jake.

"With my son monopolizing your time from the minute you came into the house, I never got to ask you how the walk over here went. I didn't have you over to answer a hundred questions and practice baseball with him."

"Then why did you have me to dinner?" A strand of her blond hair had worked its way out of her ponytail and enticed him to smooth it behind her ear. He balled his hands to keep from following through on that impulse.

"To help you get out more and feel like you won't have a panic attack. But also to have food other than from a can or a frozen box."

"I'm not starving. I do have a list of places that deliver food when I get tired of frozen dinners." He couldn't resist the temptation any longer. He brushed the stray lock behind her ear. The silken feel of her hair sliding over his fingertips made his stomach quiver, his breath catch.

Her gaze was riveted to his and for a long moment they looked at each other. She finally broke the silence, saying, "I love to cook." Her voice quavered, and she paused, glancing away. "My husband enjoyed my cooking. I miss that. Josh only wants a simple meal like pizza, spaghetti, macaroni and cheese. I don't get to experiment with new recipes the way I did when Sam was alive."

"You can experiment on me anytime. I know it's a tough job, but I think I can handle being your taster."

"Then you have a standing invitation to come to dinner Sunday night when Josh is at the youth group at church. That way I won't subject him to any of my fancy gourmet dishes."

"I can't let you do that."

"You'd be doing me a favor. I'd be elated to spend some quality time in the kitchen."

The thought that he could give her joy made

him smile. There was so little of that in his life lately. "Then I'll be here. Same time as tonight?"

"Yes. Craig's mom is driving the boys to church on Sunday so I'll have plenty of time to wow you with my culinary skills."

"After the food I've eaten in the army and here, it won't take much. I used to appreciate good food, but I'm more like Josh lately. Just something simple that doesn't require a lot of thought or work on my part."

"But that's the beauty of this invitation. You won't do either. I will and I'll enjoy doing it. There's something creative about coming up with a dish that is delicious and different from the usual."

"If you feel that way, why didn't you train to be a chef? Why a veterinary assistant?"

"Because I love animals more. There was a time I contemplated being a veterinarian, but I got married between my second and third year in college and had Josh about a year later. With my husband having to finish his last year to get his engineering degree, we didn't have the money." She stared at her lap, her hands clasped together. "After that, there never seemed to be a good time to go back to school, especially with Sam's seizures becoming worse."

Jake couldn't see her expression well with her eyes glued to her lap, but he heard the pain in her voice and saw the stiff set of her body. Laying his hand over hers, he wished he could take her hurt away. "I'm sorry. I shouldn't have asked. It's none of my business."

She shook her head. "No, I consider you a friend. What I was going to add is that I've found something I really love doing, training dogs to help others. I'm not sure I was cut out to be a vet like Dr. Harris. He's a great boss and handles the bad things that happen to animals so much better than I do." When she lifted her head and peered at him, she was calmer, her expression neutral. "How about you? What made you go into the army? Josh told me you went to college and got a degree in psychology?"

"My father was a career military officer. I thought I would work on my master's and possibly my Ph.D. while I was moving up the ranks in the army. Then when I retired, I would have a profession. All my life that was what was expected of me: to follow my father into the army."

"And you regret now that you can't?"

"No, but I'm not the person I was. That's one of the reasons I didn't want to live in Florida where my father and his second wife are. He sees me one way, and that Jake died the day of the ambush."

"That's understandable when you have a major trauma occur. Ben feels a lot like that."

He didn't look at Emma. He couldn't. When he'd been with his father the last time, he'd seen the disappointment in the general's expression. Jake was being discharged because of his injuries, and he didn't fight leaving the army. In the general's book, he was giving up.

"Maybe your parents were more understanding about what Ben was going through. My dad wasn't. He never said it, but I think he thought I was weak. A man in the Army Special Forces is supposed to get patched up and keep going, return to the field and fight another battle."

Emma touched his hand, stroking it before she curled her fingers around it. "I'm sorry. How did he expect you to keep going with your leg like it is?"

"I was supposed to take a desk job in Washington until I was fully recovered. The general has a lot of pull. If I had wanted, it would have happened, however long it would have taken for me to get back the full use of my leg."

Using her forefinger, she turned his head so he looked right at her. "You answer to yourself and God. Not anyone else. You have to ask yourself what you want. Not your father. Not anyone else but you."

His eyes slid closed for a few seconds. "I've never said any of this out loud. How do you do it—get me to talk about something I'd just as soon forget?"

"One of my many talents." One corner of her mouth tipped up. "Seriously, people do need to talk to someone about what's bothering them or often it makes the situation worse. Not speaking about it doesn't make it go away, no matter how much we wish it did."

"You sound like you know this firsthand."

"Yes, but I haven't taken it as far as you have."

"You haven't said anything to anyone? You've kept something painful to yourself?"

She nodded, slipping her hand to his upper arm to keep the physical connection in place.

"Forget about the mess I'm in. I do have a master's degree in psychology. Maybe I can help you. At least I can listen."

She checked her watch. "Oh, look, it's getting late. I need to make sure Josh has finished his homework. It's nearing his bedtime."

In other words, she didn't trust him with what was bothering her. The thought hurt Jake after he'd revealed nearly everything to her. At least he didn't tell her how he felt he was pathetic; that part of what his father said was true. He should be able to bounce back and live a normal life, even if it was as a civilian.

He stood and signaled for Shep to do likewise.

"We'll be going. Thanks again for a delicious meal. I'll see Josh tomorrow for his self-defense." He started for the porch steps.

"Jake."

He kept going as though she hadn't said his name in almost a plea for understanding. "Good night."

Even though it hurt his leg to move as fast as he did, he strode toward the sidewalk, holding Shep's leash, refusing to look back. Somehow he knew she was still watching him.

When he rounded the corner and walked down Park Avenue, at first he didn't see the front of his house, but as he grew closer, a chill flashed down his spine. In the glow of his porch light he saw that the large glass window in his living room was shattered.

Jake's gaze fastened on the destruction, and he flashed back to the village in the mountains with its windows and doors blasted out, debris and carnage lying everywhere. Fallen buddies. Civilians caught in the crossfire. Huts destroyed.

The sounds of gunfire inundated him. The moans and cries of suffering soldiers and villagers filled his mind.

He quaked, his heart racing. Sweat poured off his face. The noise of war all around him and even the scent of gunpowder assailed him.

Bark! Bark!

Something wet and cold nudged his hand over and over.

Another yelp, followed by more, demanded his attention.

Jake looked down and saw a large dog rubbing himself against his leg. No, his dog. Shep.

He blinked and knelt, putting his arms around the German shepherd. He clung to him as though his life depended on the dog.

Time passed. He had no idea how long he sat on the sidewalk in front of his house, holding Shep, feeling the dog's calm breathing, his warmth chasing away the cold that encased Jake.

Finally, when the trembling eased, Jake felt his thoughts clearing, bringing him back to Cimarron City. Safe. No enemy was waiting behind a building to shoot him. No more rocket launchers were annihilating buildings or transport vehicles.

Then he glanced toward his house and remembered the window. Had someone broken in? If he went inside and found someone there, he didn't know what he would do. He dug his cell phone out of his pocket and called 911.

Chapter Seven

As Emma finished cleaning up the kitchen after Jake left, she reflected on what he had told her about his father. It had taken Ben months to start talking about what he was going through, and once he did he was more open to therapy to help with the PTSD. She hoped it was the same with Jake because...

What? I'm attracted to him? She didn't want to be. She'd dealt with her husband and his problems and was glad she could be there to help him, but in the end she was the reason he was on the ladder that he fell from. She couldn't be responsible for someone else that way. But she could be a friend to Jake and help him when he would let her.

The ringing of the phone startled her, and she gasped. She dried her hands and hurried to answer it.

"Emma, this is Marcella. I was going to bed

when I saw a police car outside Jake's house. I thought I would let you know. I'm heading over to his house right now."

Emma wasn't sure what was going on, but Jake probably didn't need a lot of people showing up at his house. "Let me check on him and Shep, then I'll give you a call."

"Promise. No matter how late."

"I will." When she hung up, she rushed to Josh's room to let him know where she was going. "The police are at Jake's house. I want to make sure he's okay."

Josh shut down his computer. "I'm coming with you."

"You'll need to stay out of the way. Maybe on his porch until I know what's going on." Emma began imagining all kinds of scenarios, causing her breathing to become shallow until she was panting as she headed out of her house.

A few minutes later, Emma approached Jake's place as the police officer was leaving. They passed on the sidewalk, her attention trained on Jake in the doorway with Shep right next to him. He looked all right. Relief flowed through her the closer she came to Jake, and she didn't see any signs of a panic attack.

"Mom, look at his window." Josh pointed toward the one in the living room that faced the street.

She mounted the stairs to the porch, her eyes

returning to Jake's. Beneath his calm expression she spied a hard glitter in his eyes for a few seconds before he masked it. He was holding himself together, his hand on top of Shep's head.

"Marcella called to tell me the police were at your house. We were worried. I told her I would find out what happened then let her know."

"What happened?" Josh waved his hand toward the window. "Someone rob you?"

Jake stepped back. "Come in." As he walked toward the living room, he continued, "I couldn't find anything missing. The officer thinks it was a prank. There were several large rocks found on the floor. He took them to see if they could pull any prints from them. But he wasn't hopeful."

Entering, Emma peered at the glass all over the carpet, a cool breeze blowing in from the gaping hole. "I'll help you clean this up. What are you going to do about the window tonight?"

"I hadn't thought that far. Tomorrow I can get it replaced but I'm not sure…" Jake stared at the large, shattered pane.

"We've got two sheets of paneling in our garage we didn't use when redoing the den. They'll cover most of the window. Josh and I can go back home and bring them. They're pretty big so it might take two trips."

Jake looked at her son still taking in the destruction. "I can help. Maybe between the two of us, we can do it in one trip. What do you think, Josh?"

He nodded, his chest puffing out. "They aren't that big. We can do it together."

Emma looked at Jake. "Are you sure?"

"Yes, my trip home earlier went fine. But I'm leaving Shep here with you."

"No, I'll be fine."

"This isn't up for debate."

She started to argue with Jake, but the determination in his expression told her it would be useless. "Where's your vacuum cleaner?"

"In the hall closet." Jake put his hand on Josh's shoulder. "Come on, kiddo. You can even help me nail the boards up."

"Wait, here's my key." Emma passed it to Jake.

"Good thinking."

His chuckles sprinkled the air and made Emma smile. She quickly called Marcella and told her what happened then retrieved the vacuum cleaner. After she picked up the large pieces of glass, she swept the carpet over and over and then straightened a metal lamp that had been hit.

Shep barked as the guys returned with both sheets of paneling. Josh's face beamed, and Jake seemed all right, his expression even. Then he focused on her, and a light gleamed in his eyes, warming her.

"I appreciate these panels. Otherwise, I might have had to sleep on the couch to make sure no one tried to come through the window." Jake greeted Shep, rubbing him behind the ears.

"Those jagged edges probably would be a deterrent for most rational people, but I have my doubts about anyone who goes around doing this." Emma wound the cord on the vacuum cleaner.

"Mom, I'm gonna help Jake put these up. Okay?"

She glanced at her watch. "Only if you agree to go right to bed when we get home."

"I can manage without—"

Emma waved her hand. "No, we're staying and both of us will help you. The job will go faster."

"Then I'll go get my nails. I think there are two hammers in the garage." He started toward the hallway, stopped and glanced at her. "Did you call Miss Kime?"

"Yes. Don't be surprised if she isn't over here first thing in the morning."

When he disappeared from view, Josh moved closer and asked quietly, "What if this is Liam and Sean getting back at Jake? He did stop the fight. Liam went to the principal's office at the end of class today. What if they do it to us, too?"

"Stop. You can't worry about what might happen. Worrying is wasted energy. If someone does something, we'll call the police and fix the window, just like Jake's doing."

Josh frowned. "Liam gets away with so much. He's sneaky."

"It'll catch up with him. Sandy and I are rallying the moms. And Mrs. Alexander and the principal are aware of the situation. They don't support any kind of bullying."

"Tomorrow Jake's gonna work with us."

In less than two weeks Jake had become important in their lives. But he had his own problems and didn't need to be burdened with theirs. She never wanted Jake to regret knowing them. She knew how fragile his world was.

Lord, if this is the work of Liam and his buddies, please bring them to justice. They need to be held accountable for their actions. Too many people have been hurt by them.

When Jake came back, carrying his supplies, quivers flashed up her spine. He had a commanding presence that kept drawing her to him.

"Here we go. Two hammers and enough nails to put these panels up. Who wants the extra hammer?" When Josh's arm went up, Jake gave him the tool. "You can nail the bottom part while I do the top."

"What do I do?" Emma asked as the guys walked out onto the porch, the lighting still bright enough to work.

Jake gave Josh a look that said they would tolerate her assistance. "Supervise."

"I can at least help hold it up until you get enough nails in the panel, and if you need more nails, I can give them to you."

"Sure, Mom, that's a good job for you." Josh and Jake shared another look, accompanied by her son's rolling his eyes.

"On second thought, I think I'll take Shep out back. You two can do some male bonding."

Josh giggled.

Snorting, Jake started hammering.

In the backyard, Emma sat on the top step while Shep went around sniffing the ground. This was what she wanted, her son bonding with a man. There were times she couldn't help Josh the way a male could. But was this what Jake wanted? Having a young boy looking up to him, wanting his opinion? Was he willing to listen to Josh's problems while he was wrestling with his own serious issues?

Finally, Shep trotted to the stairs, mounted them and sprawled across the deck next to her. "Hey, boy, how are you liking your new home?"

In answer he rubbed against her then hopped to his feet and ambled to the back door. After a series of barks, Jake let him in. While Shep pranced in as though he owned the house, Jake locked looks with Emma.

He stepped back from the doorway and called out, "Be back in a minute. I need to talk to your mom."

She turned toward him and watched him shrink the distance between them in three long strides. His limp was more pronounced after a long day.

Clutching the railing, he lowered himself down next to her. "You've got a fine son. You've done a good job with him."

"I don't always feel that way." She shivered more from the silky thread of his words than the cool breeze blowing.

"Cold?"

She nodded, not sure she could adequately explain she was but wasn't.

He slipped his arm around her and pulled her closer. "We talked about tomorrow with his friends coming over. He wanted to know if I was sure I wanted to do it. Did you tell him I am suffering from PTSD?"

"No, there isn't any reason to. But I'm sure he knows something is going on. He's a smart kid." She turned until their gazes linked, their faces only inches apart. "He knows about his uncle Ben, and it hasn't affected how he feels about him. You aren't less of a man because of it."

"I feel like I am."

She wanted to say that was nonsense, but he wouldn't believe her. Her brother hadn't. Once her husband had basically said the same thing after a severe seizure. Still, she went on, "PTSD isn't who you are. That doesn't change, not the core essence of you. The same was true of Sam with his seizures. They were something he had to deal with, but they didn't make him who he was."

Jake studied her face. "I appreciate what you're trying to do, but—"

She stopped his words with her fingertips pressed against his mouth. The physical contact with him captivated her, the softness of his lips in contrast with the day's growth of beard on his chin. Her throat went dry. Her pulse accelerated.

"I'm only telling you the truth," she murmured, his head bending closer.

She wound her arms around him, wanting him even nearer. This was the first kiss she'd shared with a man since her husband died, and it felt so right. A scary thought. What was she doing? She wasn't ready for any kind of relationship with a man when she was the reason her husband died.

She pulled back. "I need to get Josh home. It's a school night. Sandy is bringing all the boys over tomorrow at four-thirty. I'll be here at five to help and then take them home later." She pushed to her feet, her legs shaking. "Is that all right? If not, what sounds good to you?" Her words flew out of her mouth so rapidly she could hardly follow herself.

All emotion fled his face as he rose and crossed to his back door, letting her go inside first. "Whatever works for you all. I'll be here."

She blocked his way into the hallway. "I won't ever tell Josh about your PTSD. If you want him to know, that'll have to come from you. In Josh's eyes his uncle Ben was the greatest before he was injured and still is now that he knows the problems Ben has."

"How did you explain Shep?"

"He thinks Shep helps with your leg. I train all kinds of dogs—service, therapy, companions. If I'm not needed at the animal hospital, I'm working with a dog. Dr. Harris is one of the supporters of Caring Canines." She made her way to the living room, feeling the drill of Jake's look as she walked ahead of him.

"Ready, Josh?"

Her son nodded, whispered something to Shep and rose from the floor. "I finished nailing that last piece of paneling. See ya tomorrow, Jake, Shep."

"Thanks, kiddo, for helping me."

Josh grinned and waved goodbye then headed down the porch steps.

Emma hung back, wanting to explain why she'd broken off the kiss. But the words wouldn't form in her mind. She couldn't tell him about her part in

Sam's death. Instead, she mumbled, "Good night," then hurried after her son.

Jake watched Emma and Josh leave, replaying in his mind the sensation that had swirled through him when he'd kissed her. Then the feeling of rejection when she had yanked back as though he was damaged goods. And he was. He wasn't whole, no matter how much she tried to reassure him he was, that his PTSD had nothing to do with his masculinity.

It wasn't true. It controlled his life. He sometimes felt like a prisoner.

Anger surged through him. He slammed his door so hard, the pictures on the walls in the foyer shook.

I want to be whole. I want my life back. Lord, help me.

Chapter Eight

Saturday afternoon Emma wrote a check to the hospital, draining the last of their funds for the month, but at this rate she would have it paid off by the end of the year. That would be a good feeling, and her next payday was in a few days.

Josh came into the living room, beaming. "Mom, you should've seen us with Jake today. We were awesome. I learned two new moves."

Emma basked in the expression on her son's face. Since Jake had been working with Josh on his baseball skills and self-defense moves, she'd seen more smiles and joy in his eyes. "I was impressed when I saw you all on Thursday working with Jake."

"He told us today you aren't a snitch if you tell the authorities a crime's being committed. That we all need to stand up to someone who's doing something wrong. He told the guys about when he was bullied and what he learned from it."

"What was that?"

"Letting the bullies get away with it only encourages them to do more."

"True, but I don't want you starting any fights."

"He doesn't believe in that, either. He says as a group we should stand strong."

She imagined if Ben were here he would be telling her son the same thing. She was glad Josh had Jake to turn to. "He's going to be here any minute. Are you ready to go to the ranch?"

Josh's smile grew. "Yeah. I get to show him the dogs at Caring Canines. Can I take Buttons? Jake said Shep was going with him."

"Sure, but on a leash."

Josh whirled around and raced back to his room to get the leash then went to the backyard for his terrier.

Emma rose from the desk and rolled her head around, then stretched, trying to work the tightness out of her muscles. She hated balancing the checkbook, but at least it was done for the month. Now she intended to have a nice day at Winter Haven Ranch with Jake and Josh.

Glimpsing Jake pull into the driveway in a blue Ford Fusion made her heart seem to pause in her chest then begin pounding faster than normal. This was a first. He was driving her and Josh to the ranch. She knew he drove when he went to the doctor or a few other required places, but this trip was for fun. It was just an opportunity for Jake to get out more with Shep and spend some time with her and Josh.

Like a family popped into her mind, and she quickly brushed it aside. Jake was a client she was helping adjust to the service dog she'd trained. But in her heart she knew Jake and Shep had bonded and didn't really need any help from her.

"Josh, Jake's here. Let's go!" she yelled and grabbed her purse.

Her son hurried from the back of the house with Buttons on a leash. "Do you think he'll mind her going?"

The doorbell rang. "We'll ask him." Emma moved to open the door.

Seeing Jake standing on her porch rather than honking for them to come out sent her heart racing again. She imagined him in his dress uniform, and her legs went weak with the picture in her mind. He would have been impressive.

"Hi, we're ready," she said with a grin that matched his.

"Good. I've heard a lot about this place. It'll be nice to finally see it." Jake glanced at Josh. "Do you want to take Buttons?"

"Can I?"

"Sure. Let's go." He stood to the side while Emma and Josh left their house, then he followed them to his car, opening the front passenger door for Emma. "Josh, you can hop in with Shep in the back. I figure you can keep the dogs entertained. I hear you're good at working with them."

Josh blushed but drew himself up tall. "I wanna train them like Mom."

When Emma settled herself in the car, she glanced back to make sure Josh sat between the two dogs. Shep was thoroughly trained, but Buttons had only started. She lay down and placed her head on Josh's lap as if staking her claim to him.

"Josh was telling me the lesson this morning went well. I know the other parents are happy with what you're doing."

He glanced at her then backed out of her driveway. "The boys are eager to learn." His gaze slid to her again, a gleam in his eyes. "I've been enjoying it."

"Did you ever hear anything back from the police about your window?"

"They managed to pull a print off one of the smooth rocks, but nothing turned up in their database."

"That's because it was Liam," Josh said from the backseat.

"What makes you think that?" Jake stopped at a red light, his knuckles white as he gripped the steering wheel.

"Because I heard him bragging about toilet-papering someone's house where he used to live. He likes to do stuff like that," Josh answered.

Emma twisted toward her son. "That's not the same thing. I don't want you saying anything without proof."

Josh tilted up his chin. "It was him. I know it."

Emma chanced a look toward Jake, trying to read his expression. Tension poured off him, but she wasn't sure whether it was because they were talking about the other night or the fact he was driving. She shouldn't have brought it up.

He'd warned her that driving for him was hard. Did a piece of trash in the road hide a bomb? Would stopping at a light invite a sniper's shot? He had to keep reassuring himself he was home and safe.

His chest rose as he dragged in a deep breath. Jake started across the intersection. "Josh, I'm pretty sure it was Liam or one of his friends, too. Since the police haven't found them, they'll start to get reckless and mess up. They'll be caught. Until then I wouldn't waste any energy thinking about it. I refuse to let someone like Liam ruin today."

"Okay," Josh said. "But when do ya think he'll get caught?"

"In time." His tight grip on the steering wheel loosening some, Jake turned onto the highway that led out of town. "So what are we going to do first?"

"Caring Canines," Emma and Josh said at the same time.

"Not the horses? I've heard that Dominic Winters is building up his herd."

"When I go to the ranch, Madi and me like to ride. Once we went to the factory Dominic built on part of the ranch."

Emma frowned. "You never told me. That's pretty far from the barn."

"We just went to the hill overlooking the factory. Chad went with us. I think Madi bugged him until he did."

"Who's Chad?" Jake drove through the gate to Winter Haven Ranch, the stiffness in his shoulders relaxing.

"The foreman. Madi has him wrapped around her finger. He lets her do a lot of things." Josh's forehead creased. "Maybe I should find out how from her."

"Maybe I should say something to Abbey," Emma said with a chuckle.

"Mom! You better not. Madi will get mad at me."

With laughter in his eyes, Jake looked at Emma. "So how old is this Madi you keep talking about?"

"Ten. She's not like most girls. She's cool."

When Jake parked in front of the building that

housed Caring Canines, Josh grabbed Buttons and scooted out of the back of the car.

"He likes coming out here." Jake watched Josh hurrying into the building.

"Yeah. Madi and Josh have grown closer since Abbey and I have been working together to get this place going. Don't tell my son, but Abbey says that Madi has a crush on him."

"Probably a good idea. At that age, I didn't have any interest in girls."

She shifted toward him. "So, Jake Tanner, when did you acquire an interest in the opposite sex?"

"Oh, about eighth grade when the most popular girl asked me to the dance at the end of the year. How about you? When did you become interested in boys?"

"Ah, I remember it as if it were yesterday. Keith Chambers moved to Tulsa, and the first day he walked into my sixth-grade class, I thought it was love at first sight. Sadly, he didn't. We did become friends by the end of the year."

"See? Girls seem to be into that much earlier than boys."

"Because we figure out way before you all that love makes the world go around."

His laughter filled the car. It wrapped around her as though his arms embraced her.

"What a cliché."

"But true. I'm not just talking about a man and

a woman. I'm talking about friendship, family, the Lord. Love is what it's all about. Even when I become attached to a pet, that's a form of love. I don't want to do anything halfheartedly."

"So you either love something or someone or what—hate? Isn't that the opposite of love?"

"I don't think there has to be an either/or. I look for ways to heighten my good feelings about something—someone." *Is that why my feelings for Jake are shifting?*

He leaned toward her, hooking a stray strand of hair behind her ear, then cupping her face. His brown eyes delved deep into hers, assessing, probing for answers. *Where do I stand with you?* Her heartbeat picked up speed.

"My grandma used to tell me that God is love and love is God." The rough pad of his thumb made circles on her cheek, sending chills through her.

She swallowed hard. "She's right. Marcella and your grandmother were good friends. I can remember when she died last year how heartbroken Marcella was."

"I didn't get the news of her death until a week later. I was on assignment behind enemy lines. The first thing I did when I came here to live was go to her grave site and say goodbye." He glanced away. "I fell apart when I saw it. She understood me and was always there to support my decisions.

I refused to go to West Point the way my father, her son, wanted. My dad and I had a huge fight over it. That summer between high school and my first year in college I stayed with Grandma. My dad didn't speak to me for months. I wasn't sure if I wanted to go into the service. I was eighteen and needed more time to think about my future. In the end, after I completed my bachelor's degree, I did sign up but my father was always disappointed I didn't go to West Point."

"I'm so sorry. I know it's hard when parents have one vision for us and we have a different one. Mine didn't want me to quit college so I could work and put Sam through his last year. I don't regret doing that one bit, but they thought I was putting my dreams on hold." She covered his hand, and his look connected with hers. "I love what I'm doing, and I might never have stumbled across training dogs if it hadn't happened the way it did. Now my parents understand, especially when they see how Ben is with his service dog."

"I wish I could say the general will understand one day. He won't. The army is his life, and he thinks one way or another it should be mine, even with this injury." His hand tensed under hers.

"What are you doing about the medal they want to give you? Veterans Day is only a couple of weeks away."

"I don't know if I can accept it. I…"

Someone banged on the window next to Emma and she jumped, swiveling around to find Abbey and Josh standing next to the car. "A lot of things can change by then. Give it some more time. I think we're being summoned." She pointed her thumb at the two. "I'd like to introduce you to my best friend."

When she started to open the door, he grasped her hand and stopped her. "Thank you. I appreciate what you've done for me."

I want more than gratitude. The words were on the tip of her tongue, and she swallowed them. Being friends was all that Jake could handle or want. She would have to settle for that, especially since she wasn't sure what she wanted anymore.

When she climbed from the Ford and Jake joined her, Emma made the introductions while Abbey and he shook hands. Then Josh grabbed him and tugged him toward Caring Canines.

Abbey gave a low whistle. "Good thing I already found my man, or you'd have competition."

"For what? We're friends."

"Girlfriend, what I saw on his face when I approached the car didn't look like friendship to me."

Emma blew a breath, lifting her bangs on her forehead. "No, it was only gratitude. Nothing else." Then she walked after her son and Jake before her best friend had them engaged and the wedding planned.

* * *

Jake watched Madi and Josh racing toward the black barn with a bichon and terrier right beside them. Josh wasn't going full speed probably in order to allow Madi to keep up. All around Jake were green pastures, black fences and horses. He spied a foal next to its mother nursing in the paddock next to him. There was something about the scene that calmed him.

"From what you've told me about Madi, she's doing remarkably well since the plane crash." Emma walked beside him, and Jake fought the urge to slip her hand in his. It would send the wrong message. All he could handle was the friendship she offered.

"Her injuries involved both of her legs. She had to really work to get where she is today, but she was determined. I have been amazed, but then I think a lot of it had to do with Cottonball, Abbey and Dominic."

"So that fluff ball of fur was her therapy dog?"

"Yeah, a stray Dr. Harris found. She hadn't been on her own long, thankfully. Madi fell in love with her and the rest is history."

"I see a black Lab at the barn. I think there are as many dogs here at the ranch as horses."

Emma chuckled. "Not quite but who knows in the future. Abbey has ambitious dreams about

Caring Canines. She wants her dogs to help people not only around this area but all over the region."

A tall, dark-haired man came out to greet the children. "Is that Chad, the foreman?" Jake slowed his step, his leg aching from walking so much this afternoon, as well as the self-defense lesson in the morning. He wished he'd brought his cane.

"That's Abbey's husband, Dominic. She told me he'd meet us down here. She thought it would be fun for the kids to go riding."

"And us?"

Emma smiled. "Yes, unless you want to stay back."

His expression brightened. "I haven't ridden since I was a teenager, but I used to love it when I went to my grandparents' farm in Virginia."

"Your mother's parents?"

"Yes, my mom's father was an army man, too, but he was in only four years. Not like my dad's family who all made long careers in the military."

"Was your dad's father a general, too?"

"Yes." Jake came to a stop.

Emma stepped in front of him, and her gaze drew his. "You did your part for eight years. You did all you could. You've done nothing wrong. Isn't the army wanting to give you one of its highest awards an indication of that fact?"

Shep planted himself right next to Jake, his body pressing against him. Automatically, Jake's hand went to the top of Shep's head. His throat thickened. His eyes blurred when he peered into Emma's beautiful face. "Why was I one of the soldiers to survive? I rarely leave my house. I…" As usual, he couldn't completely express what he was wrestling with deep inside. Although it hurt his leg, Jake knelt to stroke Shep's back, relishing the calmness that washed over him when he did.

Emma stooped next to Jake, laying her hand on his arm. "You aren't the only one who feels guilty about surviving. Ben went through the same thing when the soldier he was with died. My husband should never have died. He shouldn't have been up on that ladder. He—" Emma clamped her lips together.

"He what?"

She closed her eyes for a second. "This conversation is about you. Not me."

Like Jake, she could share only so much before she shut the door on what was going on inside. But that didn't stop him from wishing she would say more.

"Mom, aren't you two coming?" Josh called from the entrance into the barn.

She rubbed her hand up and down his arm. "Are you up for riding?"

Jake glimpsed over Emma's shoulder the eagerness in the kids' eyes. "Actually, it'll be a relief not to walk for a while."

"Okay. I see Abbey coming." Emma rose.

"I'll be there in a moment." Jake watched her move away from him, the whole time his hand gliding over Shep, the soft feel of fur beneath his palm.

He cared for Emma. He needed to pull back emotionally from her. He didn't want to hurt her. He had nothing to give a woman, and she deserved so much.

He struggled to his feet as Abbey neared. He'd talked to her earlier about the PTSD therapy group but hadn't said he would do it. He was nervous. Accepting the dog was one thing but once he participated in a group specializing in PTSD, he was admitting out loud that he needed intensive help.

Abbey smiled at him and paused. "Are you going to ride with us?"

"Yes." He started toward the barn with her. "You have quite a nice training facility with Caring Canines."

"I couldn't have done all of it without Dominic, my father and Emma. They all helped me tremendously. Have you considered joining our group on Monday evenings?"

"I have and…" The word *no* wouldn't come out of his mouth. In that moment he realized he would deeply regret not going. Exhaling a deep breath, he murmured, "Yes, I want to."

"Great. Will you start this Monday night?"

"No, not until next week. This Monday is already full for me." He realized he should jump right in, but he couldn't go that far—not yet, but he hoped by next Monday evening he would be able to.

When Jake neared the barn with Abbey, Josh and Madi came out with their saddled horses, followed by Dominic, leading two others behind him.

He approached Jake and shook hands with him. "I'm Dominic Winters. Welcome to the ranch."

"I hear you're one of the driving forces behind Caring Canines." Jake took the reins of one of the geldings.

"I don't take any credit for it. That's Abbey and Emma and their hard work."

"Not according to the two ladies." Jake smiled.

Dominic threw a look at his wife, his eyes softening. "Supplying the money is the easy part. Josh said something about showing you the stream and woods. It's Madi's special place."

"Sounds nice." Jake caught sight of Abbey and Emma bringing their mounts out, their heads bent together as they talked.

He drew in a long breath, full of the scent of horse, earth and leather. What tension still lingered from driving to the ranch vanished.

Madi challenged Josh to a race, then both kids climbed onto their mares and spurred their horses forward. Dominic scrambled onto his gelding and hurried after the children.

Abbey laughed. "We'll spend the whole ride to the stream trying to keep up with the kids." Then Abbey mounted her horse and left with Jake and Emma still standing in front of the barn.

While Shep sat nearby, Jake swung up into the saddle and grinned. "I hope you know where this stream is."

"Yes, I've been there many times." Emma mounted her mare and came up beside him. "But I'd rather take it nice and easy."

By the time Jake and Emma arrived at the stream with Shep trotting alongside, Josh and Madi had rolled up their jeans and were walking in the water that came up to their calves. Dominic and Abbey had spread out a blanket under a large oak tree. For a few seconds Jake looked at the couple and envied their idyllic relationship. There had been a time when he'd wished to have what they had. At the moment that dream seemed unattainable.

He dismounted and tethered his horse to a branch, petted Shep for a few seconds, then made his way with Emma to the blanket. "You've got a beautiful place," he said as he eased down, using the trunk to help him. Shep stretched out near him. "Emma told me you're trimming your cattle herd and adding horses. How do you manage your ranch and a big business?"

Dominic exchanged a warm glance with Abbey. "I have a wife who looks the other way when I have to work long hours. But mostly I've got good people who work for me, which lets me grab time with my family now and then."

As Jake sat and listened to the others, their conversation occasionally sprinkled with laughter, his dream taunted him. It would never happen if he didn't admit to his problems and do something about them. Coming out to the ranch had shown him he couldn't remain hiding in his house if he wanted to get better.

"I had the best time today," Josh said from the backseat as Jake pulled out onto the highway leading into Cimarron City. "What about you, Jake?"

His headlights sliced through the darkness, making Jake realize he had stayed longer at the ranch than he had intended—and had enjoyed it. The quiet had appealed to him. "My favorite part was the ride. I'd forgotten how nice it was to be on the back of a horse."

"Yeah, I know what you mean. And the barbecue dinner was great." Josh yawned. "How about you, Mom?"

"I always love coming to the ranch. It was nice

seeing Nicholas at dinner. He's growing so fast. Before Abbey knows it, he'll be one."

Jake looked at Emma. In the soft lighting she appeared content, relaxed, luring him to join her—let everything go and relish the moment. He sighed, loosening any tightness gripping him. Today he'd come the closest to feeling normal since the ambush. His hands gripped the steering wheel. The second he thought that word a picture of the mountain village crept into his mind. He shoved it away—not wanting to go down the path that led to memories.

"So what was your favorite part?" Jake asked to keep the conversation going, his mind focused on the two in the car with him.

"The big slice of cherry pie with vanilla ice cream at the end of dinner," Emma said with a laugh. "I probably shouldn't have had it, but it was delicious."

"Yeah, that was good, but racing across the field was my favorite part." Josh's voice slurred with sleepiness.

"Mine was seeing where your mom worked and the different dogs being trained." When there was no response from Josh, Jake peered at him through the rearview mirror. "He's fallen asleep."

"That doesn't surprise me. He was up early practicing his self-defense moves and lifting those five-pound weights you gave him to use. He's taking this seriously. I usually have to drag him out of bed in the morning."

"I'm giving him a new exercise each lesson, and he's promised me he won't do it until I tell him he's got the right technique. I've been stressing that's more important than how much he lifts."

"I'm sure Josh will follow your directions, but it wouldn't hurt for me to see the exercises and the right techniques so I can keep an eye on it."

Jake came to a halt at the four-way stop sign and glanced at her, the way the streetlight angled across her features, throwing part of her face in the shadows, but not her eyes. They were trained on him. "That's a good suggestion. But not only how he does it, watch that he doesn't do it too much."

"Maybe I should take up weight lifting." She raised her arm and flexed her muscles. "I doubt you can feel much there."

He reached out and squeezed gently on her upper arm. "It wouldn't hurt."

"Is that your way of telling me I have no muscles in my arms?"

"There's a muscle somewhere in there." He chuckled. "If you didn't want me to tell the truth, you shouldn't have asked."

Headlights from the car behind flooded the Ford. Jake pressed his foot on the accelerator and went across the intersection. Two minutes later, he parked in Emma's driveway and started to get out of his car.

"You don't have to walk us to the door."

"Yes, I do."

"This isn't…"

"What?"

"A date."

"We didn't think we were going to be gone this late. Your porch light isn't on. I'm walking you to your door." Climbing from the vehicle, Jake began to skirt around the front of the Fusion when Emma hopped out and opened the back door.

A pungent, nauseating smell suffused the air. Rubbing his nose, Jake scanned the area.

"What's that smell?" Josh asked as he scooped up Buttons and trekked toward his house.

"Don't know. It seems to be coming from our…" Emma's words sputtered to a stop. Her hand clasped over her mouth and nose.

"Gross." Josh mounted the steps.

With his leg throbbing, Jake limped after Emma and Josh. "Stop, Josh."

The boy turned toward Jake.

"Let me check everything out first. Come stand by your mom." To Emma, Jake continued, "Give me the key to the house. I'll turn on the porch light. It's hard to see exactly what has happened."

Jake took the key from her trembling hand and headed toward the stairs, using the penlight he carried to scope out the area before him. Piles of trash and feces littered everywhere he shone the light. He gagged but kept moving forward to turn on the security lamp so he could inspect the damage.

Chapter Nine

Emma held her nose, trying to block the smell.
Her stomach roiled. "Josh, go back to Jake's car
with Buttons and stay there."

"But, Mom—"

"Please."

He stomped across the yard toward the Ford,
mumbling.

As he slammed the car door, the security light
flooded the porch. Jake came out of her house,
surveying the porch area. A frown carved deep
lines into his face, and he locked gazes with her.
"Do you think Josh can go to your neighbor's
while I clean this up?"

"You mean while *we* clean it up."

"In a war zone, I've smelled some pretty bad
things before. After a while, it won't be as bad."

"I've changed diapers and cleaned up after my
son got sick. We'll do it together."

"Where are your trash bags, shovel, rake, broom, dustpan and plastic gloves?"

After she told him the location of each item, she hurried to the car. "You're going to stay with Miss Baker for a while."

"This is Liam's doing."

"We'll talk about that later." She rang her neighbor's doorbell, and when Miss Baker answered, Emma explained to the older woman what had happened.

"You know I thought I heard some racket about half an hour ago—like dogs getting into my trash can when I leave it out, except that tomorrow isn't trash day so it wasn't out."

"Did you look and see anyone?"

Miss Baker shook her head. "I was watching my favorite TV show, and it was getting to the good part. Sorry." She stepped aside to let a pouting Josh into the house. "I baked some snicker doodles today. Want any?"

Josh looked back at Emma then said, "Yes, ma'am."

"It may be a while."

"Hon, don't worry about Josh and me. We'll be fine."

Emma rushed back to her house as Jake reappeared on the porch with all the cleaning items. The obnoxious smells bombarded Emma's senses, but the quicker they took care of this mess, the faster she could breathe clean air again. Jake took out his cell phone and shot some pictures of what had been done, then he placed a call to the police.

When he hung up, Emma scanned the piles of rotten food mixed in with what had to be a bag of manure dumped throughout the trash. "Someone went to a lot of trouble." On her porch wall, she spied words she wouldn't repeat spray-painted across it. That would be the next thing she dealt with.

"Yes. This isn't a prank but pure rage and intimidation."

"What are we going to do about Liam and his buddies?"

"Although we don't have any proof it was Liam, I'm going to tell the police about the boy and the motives he might have for vandalizing our houses."

"Should we wait for the police to come?"

"Yes. They'll be here shortly."

"I've run out of things to do about those boys." Frustration and anger overwhelmed her. She didn't like feeling that way, but she couldn't stop the emotions demanding release.

Jake took her hand and led her down the steps. "Let's put the dogs in your backyard. I could use some fresh air."

The feel of his fingers wrapped around hers

soothed some of the fury building in her. As they crossed her front yard, the smells lessened.

Jake slipped his arm around her shoulders and pressed her against him. "We'll find a way to deal with the boys. I hope the officer will pay Liam and Sean a visit tonight to find out where they've been."

"They'll retaliate against Josh."

"They'll try, but I'm going to work with Josh and his friends. We aren't going to make it easy for Liam and Sean to get back at them, and every time they harass us, we'll call the police. I know a couple of officers I went to school with when I lived here. I'll involve them if I need to."

When he said *we* or *us,* her tension eased a little more. She wasn't by herself, trying to figure out what to do. And she also had the Lord. There were many times in history His people were harassed and threatened, and He came to their defense. *Please help us, God. Not just for us, but for Liam and Sean. It's time to turn their lives around.*

Emma scooped Buttons into her arms while Shep walked beside Jake. At the gate to her backyard, she put Buttons down and the dog hurried away, but the German shepherd didn't want to leave Jake's side.

In the stream of light from her kitchen window, he smiled at her. "I guess he doesn't care that the place stinks."

"Think about those cadaver dogs who work with the police looking for dead bodies. If they don't mind that, the porch won't be a big deal for Shep."

Jake's laughter shivered down her—a wonderful sound she hoped to hear more and more. "And their sense of smell is much better than ours. To each his own, I guess."

His presence made her forget for a few minutes what they needed to clean up. He moved nearer and framed her face with his hands, the look in his eyes soft, appealing. "I had a nice time today. I wasn't sure how it would turn out, but I was comfortable at the ranch. I enjoyed meeting Abbey and Dominic. Madi and Josh are fun to see together, playing, kidding each other. Almost like brother and sister."

Warmth suffused her face from his caress as he brushed her hair back, his fingers combing through the strands. "I like to feel this," he said. "Until lately I didn't realize how calming a touch could be."

Neither had she. Emma wanted to melt against him, cling to him. Somehow she remained upright, but his nearness was quickly unraveling her composure. Her heartbeat hammered a mad staccato against her rib cage. Her breathing became shallow, her total focus on the man only inches from her. She wound her arms about him to steady herself.

Slowly, almost hesitantly he bent toward her mouth and claimed it in a kiss that rocked her. This man who had been a soldier, capable of taking care of her, protecting and defending, gently possessed her with just a touch of his lips against hers.

She didn't know how long she would have stayed there at the side of her house enfolded in his arms, enjoying the feel of his lips on hers if Shep hadn't barked. She blinked, dazed, trying to orient herself to the here and now.

Jake's arms slipped away from her. He leaned down and whispered, "The police are here." The words flowed over her cheek.

"Police?"

"Yes, Emma." He gave her a kiss on the forehead and began limping around to the front yard.

She watched him, reliving every second of the past ten minutes. Step by step. Touch by touch. She sagged against her house for a moment, composing herself before heading over to talk with the police. The trash on her porch didn't bother her nearly as much as before, not when she thought about the kiss Jake and she had shared.

Jake sat at Emma's kitchen table, needing to go home and take a long, hot shower to rid himself of the stench. He would when she came back from talking to Josh and making sure he went to bed. Nursing a cup of coffee, he replayed kissing Emma and wondered where in the world his brain had been. No good would come of starting that kind of relationship with her. She deserved a whole man. He wanted her friendship—and he wanted much more.

How would he back away from a woman who had come to mean so much to him? *Lord, any suggestions? One that won't hurt her.*

Nothing came to mind—except the touch of her mouth on his. If Shep hadn't barked, he would never have known the police had pulled up.

Although her footsteps were faint sounding, he heard her coming. He finished the coffee in one long swallow and rose.

"Did Josh finally go to sleep?" Jake asked when Emma came into the kitchen.

"Let's say he acted like he was, but I won't be surprised if he's still up. He had a hundred questions about what the police said, what to do about Liam and Sean. A few I could answer. Most I couldn't. I doubt the police can do much."

"At least the officer's going by both boys' houses to find out where they have been in the past few hours." Jake took his empty cup to the sink.

"I thought I would go around the neighborhood

tomorrow and see if any of my neighbors saw something. I think from what Miss Baker said, I know what time this happened." Emma crossed the room and went into the garage.

Jake followed her and stood in the doorway, watching her kneel in front of a cabinet and search it until she found a can of paint and a brush. "What are you doing?"

She glanced up. "I'm going to paint the porch."

"Now?"

"I can't have people see what's written on the wall out there." She rose.

"Get another brush. I'll help you."

"You don't have to."

"No, but it's late. If I help, it'll be done twice as fast." Jake covered the space between them and took the can and brush. "I'll be out on the porch."

She started to reach for the items in his hands. He turned away. "Jake, please go home. You've done enough. I noticed how pronounced your limp is. You're tired."

He peered back at her. "And you aren't?"

"This is my house, not yours."

"You helped me. Let me do this for you." *I need to be needed* almost came out of his mouth, the thought taking him by surprise.

"Fine, but all we have to do is cover the offensive words. Josh and I can do a proper job tomorrow. I'll have to go to the store and get some more paint. We don't have enough left in that can to redo the whole porch."

Jake hobbled toward the foyer, still stunned by what he had almost said. True, in his former life that was one of the things that had driven him: to serve and protect. But after what happened to him, he'd buried that deep inside because that meant putting himself out there with people in situations he couldn't control. The thought sent shudders down his body.

At the front door, hand on the knob, he closed his eyes, tensing for what often followed—the shakes, the sweating, the fast heartbeat, the gasps for air. Shep rubbed against his good leg. Jake peered into the brown eyes of his service dog. He sat with his head cocked as if he needed Jake to pet him, when in reality it was the other way around.

Sticking the paintbrush into his pocket, Jake hooked the can's handle over the doorknob then bent over to pay some attention to his dog. When he finally rose, he snagged Emma's gaze as she stood back, watching and waiting. The kindness in her expression reached out and took hold of him as though they were embracing again.

All tension faded.

She came toward him. His throat closed at the inner beauty pouring from her. She made him want more than ever to be well. To be the man she deserved.

He opened his mouth to say something but no words formed in his mind. He just stared at her bridging the distance between them.

Emma smiled, radiating joy. "I appreciate your help. I don't know what I would have done if I'd come home and found this without you here. Thanks."

Still no words for her came into his thoughts.

"Jake, are you all right?"

He nodded.

Tiny lines creased her forehead. "Are you sure?"

"Yes. Sorry. I was just thinking about how beautiful you are."

"Me?" She glanced down at her jeans and shirt covered with filth from the cleanup.

"Yes." He released a long breath and pivoted to open the door before he kissed her again. "When you pick up some more paint, buy a couple of motion-activated security lights. I can install them for you tomorrow." He glanced back at her and grinned. "Let's get those words covered up so we can clean up ourselves."

Sunday afternoon when Emma saw Jake carry the ladder out of her garage, she froze in mid-motion, painting the porch wall. She remembered driving up to the house and finding Sam on the ladder and before she could ask him to get down, watching him turn to see her pulling into the driveway. Then in the blink of an eye he was falling.

Emma squeezed her eyes shut, trying to wipe the memory from her mind forever. But she would never be able to because she had to live with the guilt. Why had she mentioned getting someone to put up Christmas lights?

The paintbrush slipped from her numb fingers and crashed onto the tarp-covered porch.

"Mom, you got paint all over you. And you thought I was gonna be messy." Josh laughed and continued working on his section.

She was thankful her son wasn't looking at her because her hands began to tremble. She clasped them together and marched toward Jake. "I want to put up the security lights."

"Do you know how?"

"No, but I'm sure I can figure it out."

Jake frowned. "Why should you when I do?"

"I don't want you to use the ladder." There, she said it. She couldn't tell him why; she wouldn't tell anyone.

"My leg is perfectly all right. I'm capable of climbing up and down this ladder."

She folded her arms over her chest. "I saw how you were limping after the long day yesterday."

He moved close to her—too close. "And I rested it last night and this morning. I'm fine," he said firmly.

"I don't think we need a light over the garage. We have one on the porch. That should be enough." She tilted up her chin and dared him to disagree.

"Its range doesn't cover this part of your yard. You need both of them. What's this really about?" His gaze drilled into her, straight to her heart. "I can do this, Emma."

She looked down. "These lights probably won't deter those boys, anyway."

"I'm asking again what's really…" Silence electrified the air for a few seconds. "This is about your husband falling off a ladder, isn't it?"

She nodded, finally reestablishing eye contact with him. "Please find another place to put up the security light besides over the garage."

He clasped her arm, his eyes soft. "I understand. I didn't think about that. You've got a small ladder. How about I put it on the side of the garage? I'll only be a few feet off the ground. That'll still cover your whole front yard."

"Okay. Thanks for understanding."

"Of course." Those soft eyes roamed over her face, lingering for a long second on her lips.

Instantly, the picture of her and Jake kissing yesterday replaced the one of her husband falling off the ladder. Heat flashed through her. She backed away. "I'd better get back to work so we can finish today." She still couldn't look away as she took another step toward the porch.

Finally, he did, picking up the tall ladder and going back into the garage.

Emma put her hands to her face, her cheeks hot beneath her palms. When she looked toward her son, she found him staring at her with a grin on his face. She hurried to occupy herself with completing the job and keeping her attention on her task—not Jake.

As she painted her side of the porch, Josh kept glancing at her until she asked, "What's the problem?"

He giggled. "Nothing. In fact, everything's great. Jake's a good man."

Emma averted her face, not wanting her son to see her shocked expression. "Yeah, he is."

"I know you were scared for him to get on the ladder because of what happened to Dad. He doesn't have seizures."

But he does have panic attacks. "I know."

"Then don't worry. He isn't walking around with his cane anymore. His leg's getting better."

She couldn't answer her son without revealing fears and concerns she didn't want to voice to him or Jake—or even to her best friend. To her relief her son didn't pursue the conversation.

An hour later Emma stood back at the porch to examine the finished paint job. The cream color managed to cover up the black spray paint effectively.

"Not a bad job, you two." Jake finished putting the last trash bags of the refuse from the night before in the trunks of their cars.

Josh grinned from ear to ear, highlighting the slash of cream color across his left cheek. "They aren't gonna win."

Jake settled his hand on Josh's shoulder. "That's right, kiddo. We can clean up messes and paint over graffiti."

The boy gave a thoughtful look. "We should return the trash to Liam and Sean."

Emma glanced at the PT Cruiser she would drive out to the landfill with Jake following her in his car. "I'll be glad when we don't have to smell those anymore, but we can't resort to what they do. When we do, we stoop to their low level."

"But, Mom, they deserve it."

"She's right. They'll get their due one day."

"I want it to be today."

"Yeah, it would be nice, but we have to learn patience. As a soldier, I often had to. Rushing to do something isn't always the answer."

Josh frowned. "I guess so." He peered at the road. "Mom, Carson and his mother are pulling up."

Emma swept around, greeting the two with a

smile. Neither had been at church that day. She'd thought someone might be sick in the family. As they stepped from the car, she said, "Hi, what brings you by here?"

"I wanted to tell you our house got trashed last night," Sandy said. "We've been cleaning up today. I tried calling you earlier to let you know." Sandy scanned the front of Emma's house. "What have you been doing?"

"Cleaning up, too. We just got through with painting the porch to—"

"Cover up nasty words," Sandy interrupted Emma.

She nodded. "Did you call the police?"

"We didn't see it until this morning and yes, we did."

"I did, too."

"Good. If enough people complain, something will be done about those boys."

"I'm going to call Craig's and Zach's mothers and see if anything happened to them and let them know to be on the lookout. We need to pray for Liam and his buddies. Something must be wrong for them to feel the need to do something like this."

"Mom," Josh said in a voice full of disbelief. "We should be praying they get caught and punished."

Carson said, "Yeah. They're mean."

Sandy placed her arm around Carson's shoulder. "I agree they aren't being nice, but Mrs. Langford's right. God wants us to forgive."

"How can we forget what they've done to us?" Josh scowled.

"You don't have to forget, hon. Forgiveness doesn't mean forgetting. Nor does it mean they shouldn't be held accountable."

Sandy headed toward her car, nodding toward Jake. "See you on Tuesday. Carson has been enjoying the self-defense classes."

When Sandy and Carson left, Josh went to Emma's side. "I don't know how I'll be able to forgive Liam. This all started when he moved here."

"I know it's hard, but I hope you'll try." *Can I forgive myself concerning Sam's accident? How can I expect my son to forgive if I can't?*

"Let's go out to the dump and get rid of the last of this," Jake said, cutting into her thoughts.

Josh ran toward Jake's car. "I'm riding with Jake and Shep."

"Is that okay? He'd asked me earlier and I forgot to ask you."

No, I don't want to be alone in the car with the direction of my thoughts lately. Emma faced Jake and couldn't say that. "Sure. You two just follow me." As she walked toward her car, she decided she would turn up her music loud to drown out anything threatening to invade her mind. Forgiving another was different from forgiving yourself.

Chapter Ten

"You've totally impressed me with this dinner." Sunday evening Jake relaxed in his chair in Emma's dining room. "I love pork chops, but they are even better stuffed with cranberries and apples."

"Did you get enough? I fixed extra in case you would like to take one home with you for later in the week." Emma relished the smile of satisfaction on his face. "This was the first time I prepared the side dish."

"What's in it? I know feta cheese, tomatoes and spinach but what else?"

"Orzo and pine nuts. It could be a meal by itself. A nice lunch."

"It went well with the meat, but I understand why Josh wouldn't necessarily want it."

Emma laughed. "Yeah, it isn't pizza, junk food or spaghetti."

"Best suggestion you made was asking me to Sunday dinner. I enjoyed last week's meal and this one is great, too."

"Since last Sunday we were cleaning up the porch, I had to throw something together."

"You call making chicken cordon bleu *throwing something together*? You could open your own restaurant."

"No, I couldn't. I don't have a head for the financial aspects that go with a business. I hold my breath each month, hoping that my checkbook will balance within a few dollars. If it does, then I'm happy." Emma put her cloth napkin on the table and rose.

"You don't look for the mistake so it reconciles with your bank statement?"

"Nope. I guess you do."

"Yep. It would drive me crazy if I was off."

"That doesn't surprise me. You like order." She took his plate and stacked it on hers.

"And you like chaos? I haven't seen that. Let me help you clear the table." He started to stand.

Emma waved him back. "I have crème brûlée. I don't always make dessert, but I had some extra time. I promised Josh I would save him some. This he does like. Stay right there. I'll be back in a minute."

She walked into the kitchen and scanned the

room. Pans and pots were still sitting on the stove. Ingredients were left on the countertop. She'd even forgotten to shut a cabinet door.

"Is this what you mean by chaos?" Jake asked behind her, amusement sprinkling his words.

She gave him a smile over her shoulder. "You were supposed to stay seated then you would never find out about my deep, dark secret. It'll all get cleaned up afterward, but when I'm in my creative mode, I let everything go until later."

"Then the very least I can do is help you later."

She swung around and gently nudged him back into the dining room. "Sit."

Jake glanced at Shep nearby. "Is this how she trained you?"

The dog's ears perked forward, his tail wagging.

She closed the door between the kitchen and dining room, hurried toward the refrigerator and retrieved the dessert. After she presented the crème brûlée to Jake, she sat and waited for him to take a bite.

"Mmm. I think this is the best crème brûlée I've ever had."

"This is one of my specialties. I'm glad you like it."

"I can certainly understand why Josh wanted you to save him some. Smooth. Rich." When he'd finished half his dessert, he cleared his throat. "I have a favor to ask."

"I have some extra dessert you can take home, too."

"That's good, but that isn't the favor." He swallowed hard, his jaw line tensing. "It's about tomorrow evening. Is it possible you can go to Caring Canines when I go for the therapy group? I know I've been getting out more and driving some, but I don't know what to expect tomorrow night."

"Yes and I'll ask Miss Baker to watch Josh."

"In case there's a problem?"

"Yes. I know you don't want him to know about your PTSD. He'd figure it out if he went with us."

Jake exhaled a deep breath. "Thank you. I feel like I'm saying that to you all the time."

"It's a two-way street. This week has been quiet. Maybe the police visiting Sean and Liam was exactly what was needed to make them back off."

He slid the last bite of his dessert into his mouth, frowning.

"You don't think so?"

"Usually it isn't that easy."

"Josh heard that Sean was grounded for a week."

"How about Liam?" The frown remained on Jake's face.

"I don't know about him."

"He hasn't said anything to Josh at school?"

"I made Josh promise to tell me if he did, and I've asked every day. He said no. And there hasn't been any retaliation on Craig, Zach or Carson, either."

"Then we wait and see."

She loved hearing him say *we,* but she didn't want him to feel obligated to help them. He had enough to deal with, and she felt more and more indebted. It was harder to fight her growing feelings for Jake when she felt she owed him so much. Last week when she'd seen him with the ladder, she remembered all the reasons she could *not* fall in love with the man. "This really isn't your battle."

"Yes, it is. Remember the window. That makes it my business. I'm sure Liam and Sean aren't happy I'm working with the boys." Jake pushed to his feet. "Let's clean up."

Emma rinsed the dishes and he put them in the dishwasher. She passed him a plate. "Have you decided about the Veterans Day celebration?"

"Not yet. I haven't told them no, but I want to see how the therapy sessions go. I have to feel I can do it. If I don't, I won't."

"I understand. You've got some time."

"Not much. Dad phoned today and left a message about the ceremony and medal. I need to return his call soon."

"Would he come to the celebration?"

"I hope not. I don't want him to."

Emma realized that one of Jake's problems was his relationship with his father. The man should have supported him rather than act as if Jake should be able to overcome PTSD as quickly as snapping his fingers. The general should know better because Jake certainly wasn't the first soldier to come back from combat facing PTSD. Either way, she would back his decision.

Then a thought struck her. "Does your father know about the PTSD?"

"No. I don't want him to know."

"Why? He's a soldier. Surely he knows others dealing with it. Maybe he could help."

"You don't know the general. No good would come from his knowing." The finality in his voice declared the conversation over.

Emma's heart hurt for Jake. At least Ben had their mother and father supporting him. That only reinforced her determination to be there for Jake. He needed it.

Jake observed the four boys practicing, each pair trading turns throwing the punch and blocking it. "That's a great block, Craig. The more you do it the more natural it will feel, and you'll automatically block the hit before it lands on you. Okay, I want you all to do some curls and push-ups then cool down. Class is almost over."

"It can't have been an hour," Josh said as he lay on the hardwood floor in the dining room that Jake had turned into a minigym for the boys.

Jake glanced out the picture window. "Afraid so. I see your mom pulling up in front."

"She must be early." Josh worked on his tenth curl.

"Keep going. I have to get the door." Jake made his way to the foyer and let Emma into his house. "Why the frown? Something wrong?"

"I heard back from Craig's mother, Kim, about what the mechanic said was wrong with her car this morning. Sugar in the gas tank."

"Did it happen to anyone else's?"

"No. I called to check, but Kim's car sits out in the driveway at night. The others park theirs in the garage."

Jake hung back from the dining room and lowered his voice. "Did Kim report it to the police?"

"Yes and her suspicions about Liam and his buddies. But that's just it. That's all it is—conjecture."

"Has anything happened at Zach's house?"

"So far nothing. We're going to keep each other informed of what's going on and be on the lookout, especially at night."

He took her hands and pulled her close. "They'll mess up. They're getting bolder. That'll be their downfall."

"I hope before someone gets hurt."

He moved her a few steps out of view of the boys in the dining room. "Have I told you thank you for going with me to Caring Canines for the PTSD therapy group?"

"Yes. A couple of times last night. I'm glad your first session went well."

"Listening to what others are coping with makes me able to put my experiences in perspective. When it's happening to you, you think you're the only one dealing with it." When she started to say something, he grinned. "I know Ben and other soldiers have gone through PTSD. But knowing it and really believing it are two different things. Sometimes I think I'm the only one suffering from the same nightmare or getting a panic attack because something out of the blue reminds me of the ambush."

"Yesterday I was your chauffeur. That's all. You did all the hard work."

"I slept better last night than I have in weeks—months. Shep's getting so good at detecting when my nightmares begin and stopping them. I have you to thank for that, too." Sounds from the dining room indicated the boys were finished. Jake squeezed her hands gently. "I'm glad you're stubborn and talked me into taking Shep." He backed away as Josh and his friends appeared in the doorway. "Don't forget to practice between lessons."

They all nodded.

"Thanks, Jake." Emma smiled and left with the boys trailing after her.

Jake went out on the porch to watch them walk to Emma's car. He caught sight of three kids across the street in the park, standing around, their stares trained on Josh, Craig, Zach and Carson. Jake didn't know one of the guys, but the other two were Sean and Liam. Their body language and expressions shouted intimidation.

Jake moved to the top of his steps and crossed his arms, glaring at the trio standing in the park at the exact spot where they had beaten up Josh. For a few seconds Josh reacted—fear swept down his body. Josh glanced back at Jake. He nodded his encouragement. Josh straightened, his chin lifting, his stare directed at the three guys across the street.

Emma hustled the four boys into her car and stomped on the gas, leaving the trio behind. As much as Jake wanted to go back into his house, he stayed where he was with his feet apart, his muscled arms folded over his chest. In every line of his body he conveyed a warrior stance. They stayed for only a moment more then hurried away deep into the wooded area of the park.

Jake waited another couple of minutes, then with the release of a deep breath, relaxed his tense posture. He and Shep went back inside and strode to the dining room window to look out. No sign of the trio. He didn't like the bold gesture—a taunt, really—they'd made a while ago. This wasn't over.

Lord, I know what Josh is going through. Give me the right words to say to him, to help him deal with these bullies. I haven't felt You around much lately, but please answer this request for Josh's sake, not mine.

As Jake walked toward his bedroom, his phone rang. Thinking it might be Emma, he snatched up the receiver without looking at the caller's number on the display. When he heard the general's gruff voice, he fought the urge to slam the phone back into its cradle.

"Jake? Are you there?"

"Yes, sir." He sank onto his bed.

"Why haven't you returned my last few calls?"

"I've been busy."

"Doing what? Do you have a job now?" The skepticism in his father's voice came across loud and clear.

"I'm *working* on getting my Ph.D. I want to finish within the year."

There was a long silence on the other end, and Jake was tempted to hang up.

"I got a call from General Hatchback. You're going to accept the medal on Veterans Day."

"Yes, I called him this morning." After the improvement the past month, he felt he could do it with Shep's support and the fact he would accept the medal for every man in his unit.

"Then I'll be there. I can only stay overnight, but I want to attend."

"You don't have to. It isn't a big deal. General Hatchback will give me a medal, and I'll sit down."

"Not a big deal?!"

Jake pulled the receiver away from his ear and could still hear his father. "It's an honor few soldiers receive. I will be there. That's not up for discussion."

Jake grew taut as if he had been flash-frozen. His teeth dug into his lower lip until a metallic taste coated his tongue.

"You could have gone far, son. This medal is an indication of the type of soldier you were."

"I'll see you at the ceremony." *If I go.* "Goodbye, sir."

"Jake—"

He returned the phone to its resting place before he lost his temper. He'd been taught to honor and obey the man as his father and superior in the service, but right now all he could remember was the barrier that had been between himself and the general for his whole life.

Shep jumped up on the bed and nuzzled Jake's face and neck. He put his arms around the German shepherd and thought of a childhood memory. One time his father swung him around and around. When he'd stopped, Jake had giggled and staggered, trying to catch his dad. His dad had always let him. Where was that man now?

Hours later, after eating the rest of the dinner Emma had sent home with him Sunday night, Jake sat down at his desk to work on a paper for his doctoral program. Five minutes into his trying to come up with an introduction, the phone rang. He checked the caller ID this time before answering.

"Hi, what's up?" he asked Emma, remembering the worry that had knitted her brow as she climbed into her car with the trio in the park watching.

"I went into the garage to get something out of the backseat of my car and noticed I have a flat tire caused by a nail. I've tried changing it, but I can't budge the lug nuts. It's official now. I need to start lifting weights like my son."

He smiled, peering at the blank screen on his computer. *This'll be a nice distraction.* "I can come over and change it."

"I was hoping you'd say that. I don't have a car service."

"I'll be there shortly. Do you have everything you need to change a tire?"

"Yes. At least I have that. Can't do anything with it, though. I should have had my dad or brother teach me how."

"See you in a few." After he hung up, he looked down at Shep lying on the floor next to his chair. "Boy, we need to go rescue a damsel in distress. Emma."

At the mention of her name Shep stood, his ears perked forward. Jake felt as his dog did—eager to see her. Maybe talking with her would help him forget his phone conversation with the general.

Ten minutes later Emma opened her front door before he had reached the top porch step. The expression on her face stopped him for a second. Her eyes gleaming, she radiated warmth and relief that she had him to turn to. That feeling bolstered him.

She greeted Shep with a thorough petting. "He's really the reason I call you."

The twinkle in her gaze lightened his mood even more. "I aim to please, ma'am."

"I've put on some hot chocolate—made from scratch. With the chill in the air, I thought it might be nice before you go home."

"It is the first of November."

She walked through the kitchen. "Yes, I can't wait for the holidays. Thanksgiving and Christmas are the two times my family comes to my house. They know how I feel about cooking and let me have my way. Even Josh."

"For the past seven years I was usually in a war zone during the Christmas season."

She smiled. "Then you're invited to Thanksgiving and Christmas dinner. I go all out for the holidays. It's a time to celebrate."

"I hate to intrude on family—"

"Shh, Jake. You won't be intruding on my family. I won't let you celebrate alone. Please."

He laughed. "If I don't agree, I've got a feeling I won't hear the end of it."

Emma opened the door into the garage and gestured toward a mountain of plastic containers along the far wall. "That's where I store my decorations."

"You do have it bad." When he stepped through the doorway, Jake immediately saw the flat tire on the passenger side in the back. "Good thing you caught it tonight rather than tomorrow morning when you're trying to get Josh to school and you to work. By the way, where is Josh?"

"Doing his homework. He tried and couldn't budge it, either."

Jake set to work changing the tire. "Have you been driving through a construction area?"

"No, Josh thinks it was the work of Liam and his friends today while I was at your house. Maybe that was why they were watching us leave your place."

"This kind of leak would have taken a little time. I think they were trying to intimidate the boys."

"You mean trying to tell them that no matter

how much they practice their self-defense moves it won't make a difference in the long run?"

"Something like that."

"You're probably right."

"Always."

She chuckled. "I'll remember that at least until you finish changing the tire. Then, who knows?"

Every part of him hummed with awareness of the woman standing a few feet behind him, observing him. Not one ounce of him felt uncomfortable. Actually, he liked her watching but he knew he shouldn't. He needed to be careful. He couldn't let his feelings keep developing for Emma. Not while he was dealing with PTSD.

Finished, he rose. "Where do you want me to put the flat?"

"In my trunk. I hope it can be patched. I don't have the money to buy a new one right now."

"I think it can be."

"If it was Liam, I'm glad he didn't slash my tire. That probably couldn't be fixed." She headed toward the door into the house. "You can wash up in the kitchen. I'm going to get Josh. He wanted a cup of the hot chocolate."

While she was gone, he scrubbed the dirt from his hands and tried to compose himself. He couldn't ignore his feelings for Emma. *Why, Lord? Why now when I can't do anything about it?*

He heard Emma and Josh coming and shook the

questions from his mind, busying himself getting mugs down from her cabinet and pouring the hot chocolate. "Anyone want a couple of marshmallows?"

"Me. Cover the top with them." Josh took his cup and sat at the table, with Buttons lying on the floor nearby.

"Not me," Emma said with a chuckle. "There are already enough calories in the hot chocolate. I don't need to add more."

"I'm with Josh. The more marshmallows, the better." Jake took the chair across from the boy with Shep settling beside Jake.

She set her mug down then went back to a cabinet. "I've got something for Shep. It wouldn't be fair if we're enjoying our drinks and he doesn't get anything." After she gave him a treat shaped like a bone, she eased into the chair between him and Josh.

Josh took a large swallow of his hot chocolate, a brown mustache above his upper lip. "What do you think, Jake? Was it Liam and his guys that put the nail in the tire?"

"Don't know and without proof there isn't anything we can do about it."

"I just hate that they're getting away with everything." Josh took another gulp.

"In this country a person is innocent until proven guilty. We have to respect that, but that doesn't mean we don't take steps like we're doing to protect ourselves."

Josh blew a frustrated breath out. "I can't wait until the Veterans Day celebration. Craig told me his mom said you're getting a medal for bravery."

Jake clutched his mug until his fingers ached. "How does she know?"

"There was something in the Sunday newspaper about it," Josh replied, reaching down and petting Buttons.

Jake exchanged a look with Emma, feeling trapped into attending the ceremony whether he wanted to or not.

Emma gave him a sympathetic look. "I don't get the paper. I didn't know that." She turned to her son. "How's your homework coming? It's time for bed."

"Mom, I'm old enough to stay up past ten. I still have a little."

"Then take your drink to your room and finish your work. Then to bed."

Josh grumbled the whole way out of the kitchen with Buttons trotting after him, but Emma waited until he was gone before asking, "You decided to do the ceremony?"

"I told General Hatchback I would at the end of last week as long as it was clear I was accepting for the whole unit." And before he had talked to his father or he would have said no. He would call his dad and tell him he wouldn't accept if he came. The ceremony would be stressful enough without the general there watching.

"Good. I'm glad you're doing it. I'll be in the front row, cheering you on, and I imagine the kids you're working with will be, too. And Marcella."

An extra hundred pounds seemed to weigh him down at the thought of an audience. He'd always been a private person, and this went against everything in his comfort zone. "Do many people attend the celebration?"

"I've never gone. I'm usually working, but I'm taking the day off. I want to be there to support you. You deserve this."

"No, I don't just because I made it out alive."

"That's not true. Ben told me what you did. The ones who survived did so because of you and your quick action. You're a hero. All you have to do is ask those men and their families."

Hero? He didn't feel like one. He was a man barely holding the pieces of his life together. "I still don't know about this. What if I have a panic attack during the ceremony?" The very thought sent a bolt of tension through him.

"Shep will be there. I'll be there. We'll help you leave afterward as fast as possible."

"I don't want Josh to know or the other boys."

"That you're human? That you can suffer like anyone else?"

He blinked rapidly and scooted his chair back. He started to rise when she grasped his hand and held it tight. "It'll help if my dad doesn't come."

"Will he honor your wishes?"

"I don't know. The general does what he wants. Always has and he doesn't like it when someone tries to mess with his plans. He didn't when I went to OU, and he didn't when I took the honorable discharge. I've heard him talk about PTSD before. I don't think he believes so many soldiers have it."

"Was he ever on the front line in a war zone?"

"Not that I know of. He graduated from West Point as the Vietnam War was coming to an end and by the time the Gulf War erupted he was promoted to colonel and assigned to headquarters. I know he was in Bosnia for a while before he moved to the Middle East, but again, I don't think he was involved in the actual fighting. Then he made general. Mom died and he returned to the States to be the head of a couple of different bases over the years."

She tilted her head to the side, her hand still over his, warm, comforting. "Then he doesn't know what it's like?"

"I can't say. He never talked about his job at home."

"Maybe you should ask him about his experiences."

"Don't you think I've tried? He's always managed to avoid the subject."

"That sounds like a man who hasn't dealt with something."

Jake paused to inhale composing breaths, trying to ease the tension wrapped around him. "I know. When I was getting my degree in psychology that's what I thought. I asked him about it. He accused me of psychoanalyzing him and stalked out of the room."

"When my husband died and so much hit me at once, I learned to take each moment as it came. Don't worry about the future until it's the present and happening to you."

"Isn't there something in the Bible about that?"

"God wants us to trust Him, not put all our trust in ourselves. We can't do it alone."

"I'd like to go to church with you and Josh next Sunday. I'm going to need prayers to get through the ceremony on the following day." He turned his hand over and clasped hers, then stood, tugging her to her feet. "Walk me to the door. I need to leave. You have to get up early for work."

"While you're a man of leisure, treasure each moment," she said with a grin.

"I don't want to be. I enjoy work."

She stopped in the foyer and placed her hands on his shoulders. "I understand. That's the way I'd be. I get pleasure from a job well done. When you get your doctorate, think of the people you can help, especially ones with PTSD because you have been through it."

"As this town grows, we sure could use more services for the vets here."

"Then that could be your mission."

He drew her close. "Like yours is to help provide service dogs to the people who need them."

She ran her tongue over her lips. "Yes, exactly," she said softly.

His gaze fixed on her mouth, he bent his head toward her. He wanted to kiss her again. And again. No! As much as he would enjoy every second, he would regret it later. It wasn't fair to her. He brushed his lips across her forehead, set her away from him and strode toward the door.

"Good night, Emma."

The whole way home, thoughts flew through his mind. *What were you thinking? Where is your discipline?* Now his actions probably left her more confused than ever. They sure did for him.

As he neared his place, someone wearing a dark hoodie and black pants darted across his yard, lobbing something at his house. Jake froze.

Chapter Eleven

A grenade flashed into his mind, and Jake automatically dived for cover while his heartbeat slammed against his chest. A crashing sound followed by another invaded his thoughts, zipping him back to the noise of the first explosion in the village that took out three of his men. Quaking, he felt paralyzed, trying to crawl for the shelter of a hedge. Searing pain shot through his body as he tried to breathe and couldn't.

Shep stood over him licking him, nuzzling against him—focusing him on the calming techniques he'd learned.

Then suddenly a low growl came from his dog. Jake looked up in time to see another boy running past him, wearing a dark hoodie and black sweats. In the glow from his motion-sensitive light, Jake saw Liam slow and glance back at the hedge where he lay. The boy increased his speed and disappeared around the corner.

Sweat drenching him, Jake visualized a beach with gentle waves lapping against the shore. Their rhythmic sounds soothed him as he stroked Shep.

When he was composed enough, having used some techniques he'd started learning from Abbey, he dialed the police then struggled to his feet, his legs still shaky. If he hadn't become panicky, thinking he was under attack, he could have caught the pair red-handed. Anger gripped him— more at himself than anyone else. He limped toward his house to see what damage the duo had done.

To his amazement Marcella stood in the middle of the sidewalk leading to his house, her arms crossed over her chest, a fierce expression on her face. She spied him and relaxed some of the stiffness in her posture, but her arms remained in place as did the narrow-eyed look.

She marched toward him. "I called the police. I saw two boys throw something into your house. I think they're stink bombs from what I smelled."

"Stay here, Marcella." As he neared his house to get a closer look, he smelled the noxious odor of rotten eggs coming from a hole in the new window in the living room and one in the dining room.

Putting his hand over his mouth and nose, he checked to make sure the only damage was the windows and the smell. Satisfied that was all, Jake returned to wait for the police with his neighbor.

"Did you happen to see what they looked like?" Jake moved farther away from his house and the smell.

"Yes, I did. After the problems you and Emma have had, I've been extra vigilant. Never know when this kind of behavior will spread to others in the neighborhood. I saw your light go on and went out on my porch with my video camera in case it wasn't you returning home."

"You knew I was gone?"

"Yes, sirree. Like I say, I've been watching. I've positioned my chair to keep an eye on the front of my house and part of yours."

"Where's your camera?"

She pulled it out of her pocket and gave it to Jake.

When he replayed it, he grinned. "Gotcha. Between this and my testimony, Liam and Sean will have some explaining to do with the police tonight."

"They should have to clean up the mess they made in your house."

"A great suggestion, Marcella." Jake leaned close and kissed her on the cheek. "Thank you for keeping watch." He was relieved. He hadn't been sure his identification would have been enough because he didn't actually see the face of the person who lobbed the first stink bomb.

On Veterans Day, Emma mounted the stairs to Jake's porch. The door opened. Her steps slowing, she drew a deep breath at the sight of Jake in his uniform. Wearing his dress blues, he stood in the entrance, looking every bit a soldier—distinguished, capable of protecting. But when her eyes connected with his, vulnerability lurked in the brown depths.

Since last week when Liam and Sean were arrested for vandalizing Jake's home, he'd had a couple of private counseling sessions with Abbey, who was working with Jake's doctor on a treatment plan.

Jake was determined to accept the medal for the men in his unit and make it through the ceremony without incident. He'd told Abbey about his reaction when he'd seen Liam lob something at his house, and if it hadn't been for Marcella, the boys might not have been held accountable for their actions. Until that moment she didn't think Jake fully embraced that he was dealing with PTSD. But he did now and was determined to overcome it.

"I'd whistle, but I can't very well," Emma finally said when the silence had stretched for a long moment.

"I didn't think I'd be wearing this uniform again."

"Are you and Shep ready to leave?" She had offered to drive him so he didn't have to deal with that, too.

"Shep is. I'm not sure about myself." Jake moved out onto the porch with his service dog wearing a dark blue harness with a leash attached.

"You both look nice."

"You're certainly good for a man's ego."

"I aim to please, sir."

As they got into Emma's car, Jake asked, "Are the guys coming?"

"Yes. Since I'm going early, I'm saving seats in the front row. Actually, probably the whole row since Abbey, Dominic and Madi are coming as well as Sandy, who is bringing the boys."

Red crept into his cheeks. "I'm not comfortable with all this attention."

"In two hours it will be over."

"It may not sound like a long time to you, but to me it does."

"Then let's change the subject." Emma backed out of the driveway and drove toward city hall and the park across from it where the celebration was taking place. "I understand Liam and Sean will be doing community service and going to counseling."

"Sean's parents were livid about their son's behavior and grounded him again. They're making him do chores to earn money to pay me back for the two windows. Whereas Liam's dad, with no mom around, doesn't care."

"Josh has several more boys who want to come to your class."

"Yeah, he told me yesterday at church. I'll have to think about it."

"It appears others are stepping forward to complain at school about Liam and Sean."

"If the majority won't accept bullying, it can't prevail. A few bullies against many in the end won't succeed."

Emma pulled into a parking space near city hall and the park. Because of Jake, her son wasn't as angry as before. He was smiling and laughing, not complaining about going to school. "Sandy and I have a mom's group organized and we're working with the school on an anti-bully program. After Thanksgiving they're going to have a 'Stand Up Against Bullies' day."

Jake stared out the windshield at the platform erected for the ceremony.

"Ready?"

"No. I'd like to sit here for a while. Okay?"

"Of course." She took his hand and held it, feeling his slight tremor. "I'm ready when you are. Use the relaxation techniques Abbey showed you. Keep Shep next to you. And remember you aren't alone. I'm here to support you. The Lord is with you."

More people began to arrive. The day was beautiful, the sky clear and the temperature in the low fifties. Slowly, the quiver she'd felt in him melted away, and he turned toward her.

"Why don't you go ahead and grab those seats you need? I'll be along in a few minutes."

"Are you sure?"

"Very."

Emma climbed from her car, part of her wanting to stay whether he agreed or not. But ultimately Jake would have to learn to handle his PTSD when it flared up. After crossing the street, she glanced back at him. With his eyes closed, he sat perfectly still. Was he praying? After going to church with her and Josh yesterday, he'd told her he would like to attend again.

God, he's in Your hands.

Shep, wearing his service dog vest, walked next to Jake, who took a seat on stage, scanning the large crowd. As promised, Emma sat in the front row with the four boys he worked with and her friends. He stroked the top of his dog's head while taking in fortifying breaths and visualizing himself on that beach with the calming sounds of the waves.

He'd asked to be on the program first when he had agreed. An older man slipped in behind Emma and tapped her on the shoulder. She threw her arms around him. Then Jake spied Ben coming up the aisle and sitting next to the person Emma had greeted. That must be her father. She mentioned once that Ben hoped to come to the ceremony but then hadn't said anything else. He nodded once at Ben as the high school band played "The Star-Spangled Banner." Along with Jake, everyone stood.

The mayor approached the podium to lead the crowd in the Pledge of Allegiance. When the audience retook their seats, the mayor said a few words about honoring the veterans who helped preserve the citizens' freedoms. "It is my great pleasure to have a two-star general here to give our very own hero the Distinguished Medal of Honor. Please welcome General Tanner, former Captain Jake Tanner's father, to present the award to his son."

Jake heard the words, their sound growing further away the more the mayor spoke. His heartbeat pulsated against his rib cage, increasing its thumping when he glimpsed his dad climbing the stairs to the platform. He should have known his father wouldn't honor the wishes he'd made very clear a few days ago.

As his dad joined the mayor at the podium, the world around Jake faded, noise assailing his ears but with no meaning. Beads of sweat popped out on his forehead. Shep moved closer, nosing his hand. Jake went through the calming techniques Abbey had shown him, his focus on Emma. He didn't want to have a problem in front of Josh and the other boys.

Emma smiled and rose, clapping. It took a few seconds for it to register that he was supposed to go up to the podium. He pushed to his feet, his gaze trained on Emma, his hand clutching Shep's leash. Slowly, he moved toward his father, the sound of the applause echoing through his head.

When he swung his attention to the general, his vision narrowed into a laser point. He watched his dad speak but didn't hear the words. Stopping at the general's side, Jake stood at attention while his father pinned the medal on him.

The short speech he'd written fled his mind as the crowd cheered.

"Don't you have some words to say?" his father whispered through the haze that surrounded Jake.

Jake swallowed twice then leaned toward the mike. "I'm accepting this Distinguished Service Medal in the name of the men who served under me in the Night Hawk Company." His throat swelled, cutting off any other words. He stepped back, saluted his father, then did an about-face and walked to his chair.

It took all his willpower not to keep going until he'd left the platform. Instead, he sank onto his seat. Shep placed his head in Jake's lap, and he scratched his German shepherd behind his ears, the action soothing his taut nerves.

He hadn't fallen apart—even with his father here at the ceremony. Even with the park full of people—most strangers.

The rest of the ceremony passed in a blur with Jake keeping Emma in his line of vision. She anchored him. She believed in him. He didn't want to let her down or make a fool of himself. But he wouldn't appear on stage before a crowd again anytime soon.

When the throng dissipated, Josh flew toward his end of the platform with the other three boys following. Emma hurried after them.

"Can I see it? Can I see it?" Josh and his friends crowded Jake, cutting off his view of Emma.

Carson cocked his head. "What's that in the middle of the circle?"

"The United States Coat of Arms. That's a bald eagle," Jake said, pointing at it. "And it's clutching thirteen arrows for the original thirteen states in one talon and in the other an olive branch."

Josh's forehead creased. "War and peace?"

"Yes," Emma said, putting her hand on his shoulder and moving him back to give Jake more breathing space.

"Cool." Zach's eyes grew round. "And you got this."

"Not just me. All the men in the company."

"Are they going to get a medal like this?" Craig asked.

"No, I'm keeping it safe for them." Jake looked at Emma. "Let's get out of here."

"I've got a spread set up at my house to celebrate Veterans Day. Ben and Dad are heading over there and getting the food out on the table."

When Jake saw his father disengage from a reporter and the mayor, he took Emma's elbow, moving toward the stairs. Leaning toward her, he whispered, "Who else?"

"The kids, Sandy, Abbey and Dominic. If that's too many, I can make some excuse."

"No, I'm used to them."

She glanced over her shoulder. "Should I say anything to your father?"

"No. If I know my dad, he'll be waiting for me at my house."

"Outside?" Tiny lines puckered her brow.

"No, he has a key. The house belongs to both of us." Maybe he'd outwait his father if he stayed at Emma's.

When he heard his name being called, he hurried his pace, causing his leg to ache. But he couldn't deal with the general after the ceremony. He could do only so much and keep it together. If he had his preference, he'd go home and lock the world out.

"Mom, I'm coming with you. Carson's mother will bring the other kids." Josh fell into step beside Jake.

"Uncle Ben told me that medal you got is a big deal."

Jake remained quiet, not sure what to say to Josh. The medal declared to the world that he performed heroically, but he didn't feel like a hero. He felt like a man barely holding his life together and beginning to care about someone he shouldn't.

At Emma's house, Jake hugged Ben and clapped him on the back. "It was good to see you today. Are you staying for a while?"

"Dad and I are driving back in a couple of hours. I got today off but not tomorrow." Ben smiled. "We'll be back for Thanksgiving. You haven't had a holiday meal until you've been to Emma's."

"She's had me to dinner a few times, so I know what a great cook she is."

Ben edged him away from the doorway as others began to arrive. "How's it going? It looked like Shep was helping."

"Was I that obvious?"

"I know the signs. Remember I've felt all of the symptoms." Ben moved into the dining room. "I don't know about you but I'm hungry. Hey, I thought General Hatchback was giving you the medal."

"He was."

"It was nice seeing your father give it to you. I can imagine how proud he is. Is your dad coming to the party?"

"No, but I'm sure I'll see him later."

Ben assessed his expression. "You're not on good terms with your dad?"

"No. He doesn't see why I left the military."

Ben blinked, his eyes wide. "He wanted you to stay in with a bum leg?"

"When I was hurt, his dream of my following in his footsteps vanished. Now he has a crippled son who would rather stay in his house."

"He said that to you?"

"Not exactly, but I know him. He'd go to work even when he was ill. He once said to Mom pain is part of a soldier's life. It comes with the job. He never had patience for anyone who got sick."

Ben shook his head. "Hey, man. I'm sorry. You're one of the toughest men I know."

Emma appeared in the dining room. "I figured I would find my brother hanging around the food."

"That's because I'm starved." Ben grabbed a paper plate and began piling seven-layer dip on it followed by tortilla chips.

Emma enclosed her hand around Jake's. "I want you to meet my dad. Okay?"

"I'd love to," Jake said, realizing he looked forward to being introduced to Emma's father. He'd been stationed so much of his time in war zones the past few years that he'd forgotten what it was like to live a "normal" life.

As Jake neared his house, his body tensed more with each step. Maybe his dad had had to go back to Florida immediately. But when he came in view of his place, his stomach plummeted. An unfamiliar car sat in his driveway. As he approached the porch stairs, his pace slowed.

He wasn't ready to face the general. Taking a seat on the top step, he petted Shep and stared at the park across the street. He'd enjoyed the surprise celebration at Emma's. Even with his dad's appearance at the ceremony, he'd dealt with the day's activities well. When he'd talked with Abbey at the party, she'd been pleased. Although he had not been in the midst of the crowd in the downtown park, but up on the platform, he'd been able to handle so many people in one place. And he didn't flash back once to that time in the packed marketplace in Afghanistan's capital when a bomb exploded, killing and hurting a lot of innocent people. Then not three days later, his company left for the mountains.

At the sound of the front door opening, Jake shuddered. As much as he'd prefer to stay outside in the crisp evening air, he didn't want to have a conversation with the general that the whole neighborhood might overhear. Weary, he pushed to his feet, using the railing to steady himself.

The dreaded words came out of his dad's mouth: "We need to talk."

With a sigh, Jake pivoted and made his way into his house.

"Where have you been? You can't avoid me forever."

Jake stopped in the entrance into the living room and faced the general. "A friend threw me a surprise party." When his dad flinched, he continued. "I didn't know about it until we were driving away from the ceremony."

One of his father's thick eyebrows arched. "And you didn't think I'd be here? I didn't come all this way just to give you a medal."

Jake cringed at the barb. "Since the last time I talked to you I asked you not to come, I didn't anticipate your being at the ceremony."

"That's one of the reasons we need to talk. Why didn't you want me at the ceremony?"

As much as he wished he didn't have to, Jake limped toward the couch and sank down. All his life he'd tried never to show any kind of weakness in front of the general.

"I see your leg is healing nicely. You're not using your cane." Dressed in his uniform, his father remained in the doorway into the living room, his hands clasped behind his back. He looked

every bit a two-star general in the U.S. Army—
tough, distinguished, unrelenting.

"I've been using it less over the past few weeks."

"I see you have a dog."

"Yes, a service dog. Shep."

"Why do you need a service dog if your leg is
getting better?" His father finally traversed the
distance between them and took the chair across
from Jake.

For a long moment he couldn't say anything to
the general. He could still remember when he'd
been harassed by that bully in sixth grade. No
sympathy or understanding came from his father.
Instead, his father worked with him every spare
moment, building his muscles and teaching him
to fight and protect himself. If his dad could have
added inches to Jake's height, he would have done
that, too.

"You're not one of those soldiers who thinks
having a dog will make everything better?"

Anger flashed through Jake. His willpower
stretched to its limit, he remained seated when
all he wanted to do was leave. He raised his chin.
"Yes, I am, sir."

"How can you say that?"

"Because I've seen it work for myself and a soldier in my company. It's not the only thing I'm
doing to deal with my trauma, but it is one that I
will continue. If it hadn't been for Shep, I doubt

I would have stayed at the ceremony when I saw you coming up onto the platform."

The general scowled but behind that expression Jake saw something else—susceptibility to being hurt by another—him. "How did we get to this place?"

Jake ground his teeth, waiting before he answered. "You wanted to make all my decisions. I'm thirty and perfectly capable of deciding what's best. I can't fulfill your dream for me because it isn't mine."

"All I've wanted is for you to succeed."

"Yes, in the army. I used to think that was what I wanted, but for the past couple of years I've been dissatisfied. I didn't know how to approach you about it. Now it's a moot point because I'll always have some problems with my leg when I overextend myself. A soldier needs to be at the top of his game. I've accepted I can't be."

"With that dog by your side, I'm guessing you think you have PTSD. You don't need a service dog for your leg injury."

Is that contempt in his words? Jake couldn't tell for sure. "When you've walked in my shoes, then you have a right to say what you think of PTSD. But I don't think I have it—I *know* I have it."

His father's mouth dropped open, his eyes wide.

"I've heard you say before you think it's just an excuse a lot of people use. It isn't." Jake rose before he said more. "Now if you'll excuse me, I'm going to bed."

"But it's only nine."

"That doesn't change the fact I'm tired, sir."

"I have an early flight in the morning."

"Then goodbye. Have a safe trip," Jake said in a monotone, needing the space between him and his father. Nothing would ever make a difference. He had to face it. He wasn't the son his dad wanted.

After removing his coat and shoes, Jake collapsed onto his bed, exhaustion filling every part of him. Without changing out of his uniform pants and shirt, he stretched out to relax a while…

Through the haze of gunfire, Jake spied the young boy crying, no more than four or five, coming toward him. All he could think about was the child getting killed. He rushed toward him, scooped him into his arms and hurried back to the hut he'd been using as a shelter. After he put the boy on the floor, Jake returned to the window and scouted his surroundings. With a quick glance back to check if the boy was all right, he saw the child playing with a grenade.

Jake screamed, "No! Put that down!"

In slow motion the child pulled the pin.

Nooo!

Mixed in with the sounds of the explosion were—barks?

Something scraped across his cheek. He twisted

then rolled away. Suddenly he fell, hitting something hard.

His eyes bolted open as his door slammed against the wall.

Next to him Shep continued to bark while his father charged into Jake's bedroom, fear carved into his features.

"Son, are you all right?"

Jake ached from landing on his left side. Crashing against the hardwood floor sent a shaft of pain up his leg. But that didn't dominate his thoughts. He couldn't shake the picture in his mind of the little boy playing with the grenade.

"Where did it come from? The child didn't have it on him. I would have felt it."

"Jake!" his dad shouted, kneeling next to him, grasping his arms. "What are you talking about?"

His heart racing, Jake inhaled then exhaled, the room spinning. The words describing his nightmare came out haltingly, but somehow he got to the end or at least the part he remembered.

"It didn't happen exactly like that."

"How do you know? You weren't there."

"You forget the camera on your helmet. I viewed all the footage of what was recovered from the ambush. You were wounded but giving one of your men cover as he darted toward the hut, carrying a young crying boy. When your sergeant put the child down in the hut and took his place at the other window, he left his backpack on the floor. You turned, saw the boy with the grenade and as he pulled the pin, you dived for him, grabbed the grenade and threw it out the window. It exploded a few seconds later. The aftershocks knocked you back and that was when you blacked out."

"There was a child? He didn't die?"

"No."

Relieved, Jake sagged back against his bed frame, holding on to Shep.

His dad sat next to him, and he felt the general's stare as he patted Shep. The feel of the dog's fur as he ran his fingers through it soothed something deep inside Jake, grounding him in the here and now—not the past.

"He really helps you," his father said in wonder.

"Yes. He reminds me of the present. He can sense when I'm troubled and only wants to help me. I've had him a month and yet it seems like we've been together forever."

"You always were a dog lover."

How would you know? You were gone half my childhood. But he couldn't voice that. For some reason his dad was sitting by him and something was different. "That's not it. I'm learning various calming techniques from my therapist. Shep is one of the tools I use. I don't want to be debilitated with these panic attacks, afraid to do things because I'm scared I'll have a flashback. I want my life back."

When his dad didn't say anything, Jake turned toward him. His father's head hung down, his eyes closed. He clenched his hands then flexed them, over and over.

"Dad?"

"I never wanted you to go through what I did. I've never been wounded, except in here." He tapped his temple. "I was sent to Vietnam at the end—not long before we pulled out."

"I never knew that."

"Because I never talk about it. I was so young, right out of West Point. I thought I knew what to expect in a war situation." He shook his head. "I had no idea what was in store for me. It was brutal, and I was never the same. I had nightmares and flashbacks for years." When he looked into Jake's face, his eyes glistened. "Not many for the past fifteen years. I thank God for that every day."

"You never said anything. You always seemed so together, in control."

"Because I worked hard to present that facade, especially at home, around others. I had to climb the ranks to general like my father before me. I'd been groomed for that all my life. You think I was tough on you. My father was the toughest man I've ever known. You were never to show any weakness around him. It wasn't acceptable."

Jake felt the shudder snake down his dad's body—a man who was always together. Just like his own father.

"I thought my reaction to what I'd seen meant I was cowardly, not whole, so I didn't let anyone know. I never talked it over with anyone. I wanted to but then that would have marked me as a weak man."

Jake thought about his own journey to this point. The feelings of being weak, not whole. The denial that anything emotional was wrong with him. Then he met Emma and things changed. He couldn't deny it any longer, but he still felt weak, not whole.

"When I saw you after your return, you never said anything about what was really going on other than with your leg injury. I wish you had."

"How could I when I knew I wasn't doing what you wanted me to do?" Jake's hard stare bore into his father. "You should know since you never told anyone."

"But you had the courage to. You're getting help. I didn't and the price I paid was isolating myself from my family and friends. I pushed you and your mother away. I..." His Adam's apple bobbed. "I failed you and her."

Jake never thought he would hear his dad admit he failed at something. For the first time he didn't seem larger than life, untouchable. Using the bedpost, Jake pulled himself to his feet then offered his dad a hand. "I don't know about you, but I doubt I'll get any more sleep tonight. Want to put on a pot of coffee and talk?"

His eyes softened as his dad grasped his hand and rose. "Sounds like a good plan."

Maybe we can repair our relationship—actually build one. Jake had enough to deal with. He didn't want to continue pushing his father away.

Chapter Twelve

"Now tell me why Josh isn't helping you with this?" Jake followed Emma with a grocery cart while the sound of Christmas music filled the store.

Emma grinned. "Because I thought it was about time you went grocery shopping and I needed someone to push the second cart." She paused and tilted her head. "Don't you just love the sound of Christmas music? I could listen to it all year long." She leaned toward him and lowered her voice. "Don't tell anyone but I do listen to it. Usually around April and August I need to for a week or so."

Jake laid his palm over her forehead. "You really have it bad."

"Yep, I love what Christmas stands for. Hope." During the next weeks she wanted to share that with him.

Jake scanned the aisle, crammed with other shoppers. "Why does everyone wait till the last minute to get food for Thanksgiving? Look at all the people here."

"It's like Christmas shopping at the last minute. A habit. I shop right up to the last minute for Christmas."

"I didn't take you for someone who would wait like this."

"Are you kidding? This is my second trip. I came yesterday, but my menu keeps growing. I figured you could take leftovers home with you tomorrow. Besides, I thought you could get your own groceries, too."

His eyebrow hiked. "You did?"

Jake pulled up right behind her as she searched the shelves for the spices she needed. The smile on his face caused her pulse to pick up speed. He could do that so easily to her—make her react to his presence. She was falling for him yet trying not to. If he knew he'd run the other way because he had so much to handle right now in his life. A girlfriend wasn't something he needed.

Emma waved her hand toward his cart. "You haven't chosen much for yourself."

"Dog food."

"For yourself to eat."

"I thought you were going to send home leftovers with me tomorrow."

"I am but you still need other things to eat."

He tossed a container of salt into his cart. "There."

"I hope that isn't all."

"I'll get a few other items," he said with a chuckle.

Emma moved to the next aisle, not as crowded as the last one. "You'll be bringing Marcella with you tomorrow morning?"

"Yes. Anything else I can do?"

"Nope."

Someone bumped into Jake's back. He stiffened and pivoted, stepping back. His chest rose and fell with a deep breath, then another.

The young mom with two small kids murmured, "Sorry" and rushed past him.

Jake watched her for a moment, blinked then focused on Emma.

"Okay?"

"Sure. I have to expect that in a crowded store the day before Thanksgiving. Just don't make me fight over the last turkey."

She laughed. "I've got the turkey and the ingredients for the dressing already. Now all I need is everything else."

"I'm sure my stepmom has their dinner already cooked or at least what she can do ahead of time. Priscilla is one organized woman. Like my dad. That's probably why they get along so well. Did I tell you Dad asked me to come for Thanksgiving when we talked this past weekend?"

"What did you say?"

"I'm not ready to deal with that yet—not us being together but flying on a plane. Giving control to another—the pilot."

"Haven't you figured it out yet? We don't really have control. God does." She smiled at him.

In the fresh vegetable and fruit section with more room, he pushed his cart next to hers. "Right now I get through best when I feel I have some control, some say in what happens. I know the Lord is in control of the universe, but I'm just one of billions. I doubt He's much interested in my day-to-day life."

"Why not? You're His son and He loves you."

"I know."

"Do you?"

Jake frowned. "Of course."

But the way he looked and spoke made her doubt it. She changed tactics before Jake decided to cut their trip short. "So how's it going with your father since he was here Veterans Day?" They had talked several times, but Jake hadn't said a lot about the visit.

"Awkward at first but this last call was better. It's been thirty years one way and it isn't going to change overnight, but at least now I have hope it'll improve. Just knowing he dealt with issues after Vietnam gives us a place to start."

"I'm so glad for you. A person with PTSD needs all the support he can get." Emma gathered up some sweet potatoes, then moved on to the celery and onions.

"Is that what you're doing for me? Because of Ben?"

Emma swept around, his look trapping her. "That's the way it started."

He took a step toward her. "And now?"

"We're friends. I'm doing it because of that."

"Anything else?" His earnestness charged the air.

It was as if no one else were in the grocery store. The intensity emitting from him enticed her closer. "Well, there's what you did for Josh. He's getting to be his old self thanks to your assistance. Oh, and the times you helped me to change that tire and to clean up the trash on the porch." She stared at him—couldn't look away.

"Why, Jake Tanner, it's so good to see you out and about," Marcella said, coming up and almost planting herself between them. "I'll be ready at ten tomorrow morning."

"Yes, ma'am. I'll be there to escort you."

Marcella waved her hand in front of her face as though the temperature in the store had soared. "Escort. I like that. See you then. Don't forget we need to discuss those self-defense classes for me and some of my friends." She returned to her cart. "I'm bringing the cinnamon rolls to hold everyone over until dinner is served. See you, Emma, Jake."

Emma watched the older lady wheel her basket of food around the corner before glancing at Jake. The humor in his eyes infected her, and she burst out laughing.

"I think Marcella Kime has a crush on you."

Thanksgiving Day Jake lounged in his chair at the dining room table with seven squeezed around it. Right across from him sat Emma, who had jumped up more times than he could count. This dinner had been a big deal to her—and absolutely delicious from her crunchy sweet potato casserole, moist cornbread stuffing with mushrooms and corn, lemon and herb slow-roasted turkey to his favorite— artichokes au gratin.

Ben patted his stomach. "I think I have some room for dessert. What is it?"

"I thought we'd have pumpkin ice cream." Emma pressed her lips together.

Ben's eyebrows slashed down. "What! Pumpkin and ice cream don't go together."

She chuckled, the sound light and sweet. "No, we're having something a little bit more traditional—white chocolate pumpkin cheesecake topped with shaved almonds."

"What happened to the pecan pie you have every year?" Robert, Emma's father, asked.

"I made that, too. Just for you, Dad."

"Can we have a slice of both of them?" Josh glanced from his granddad to his mom. "I'm still hungry."

"Probably because you didn't eat everything on your plate." Emma rose and gathered the plates near her.

"'Cause I was saving room for the dessert. Like Jake."

Emma started for the kitchen. "But he ate his dinner."

Jake stood, picking up the rest of the plates. "I'll help you."

"Jake, make sure my pieces are big. I'm a growing boy," Josh said as Jake left the room.

He couldn't remember having such a nice Thanksgiving—informal, full of laughter and relaxation. "What do you think of going to the park after we eat and working off some of this wonderful food?"

Emma took the cheesecake out of the refrigerator. "Doing what?"

"It's time for Josh to work on his batting. He's got throwing down pretty good. Batting isn't something we should do in your yard. We need more space. Ben, Robert and I were talking before dinner about doing something so we don't all end up falling asleep in your living room."

She swept around to face him. "You guys can help Mom and me with cleaning up."

Jake trapped her against the counter, his arms on either side of her. "Today's gorgeous for this time of year. Let's play in the park then I'll come back and help you clean up. There's no rule that says it has to be done right after we eat."

Her eyebrows shot up. "What about the leftover food?"

"We'll take care of it before we leave."

"We? You and I?"

"Yep. I may not cook well, but I can wrap food in foil and put it in containers. So what do you say?" He inched closer, her scent of lavender mingling with the lingering aromas of the dishes.

"You're not going to expect me to chase the ball, are you?"

"No, we have Ben and your dad as well as Shep and Butch."

"We have a leash law in Cimarron City."

"Then you and your mom can hold their leashes and cheer."

She cocked her head. "What's this really about?"

He shouldn't have gotten so near her. All he could do was stare at her lips with their hint of red lipstick.

"Jake?"

He averted his gaze for a few seconds. "Josh mentioned he used to enjoy playing in the park but hasn't for a while, even when a group of his friends were doing something. I think it's because of what Liam and his buddies did."

"They've been behaving lately."

"Yes, but when he thinks of the park he thinks of what happened there last. I don't want him to be afraid and stay away because of that fear."

She lifted her hand and stroked it down his jawline. "You've been so good for Josh. Yes, we'll go. I didn't realize he was avoiding the park with his friends. They used to play there a lot. I don't want what happened with Liam to taint those memories."

"Hey, you two, what's taking so long? We're starved!" Ben yelled from the dining room.

"We're coming. I think there's some turkey and dressing left. Munch on that." Emma turned toward the counter. "We'll do the park after dinner but on one condition. You'll join us this evening to decorate my Christmas tree. We always do it on Thanksgiving. Okay?"

"You drive a hard bargain, but I'll help clean up *and* decorate your tree."

He and Emma worked as a team getting the desserts and clearing the rest of the dishes from the table while her mom, Nancy, sliced and served the pie and cheesecake.

Before returning to the dining room to eat his helping, Jake captured Emma's hand and tugged her to him. "Have I told you how wonderful the meal was?"

She cuddled against him. "Yes, while you were eating, but I don't mind hearing it again."

"Well, it was. Thanks for inviting me to share your Thanksgiving. I had a frozen turkey dinner in my freezer for the occasion. I'm glad I didn't have to eat it today." In eight weeks this woman had changed the direction he was going and given him hope. His arms surrounded her and pressed her against him, and the feel of her in his embrace soothed his soul.

"Since you came this morning, you've been in a cheerful mood. Should I thank Marcella? Her cinnamon rolls?"

He smiled. "It was all you and the fact that I finished a big project for my doctorate. And one other small detail. I didn't have a nightmare last night for the first time in months."

"It was all those groceries you brought into my house yesterday. It wore you out."

"Before I know it—" he clasped her hand, enjoying touching her "—you'll be having me running laps around the park with you."

"Nope. You never have to worry about that. I don't jog or run. Maybe walk."

When they reentered the dining room, the pecan

pie and cheesecake were gone except for one thin slice of each.

Emma placed her hand on her hip. "Did you all forget the cook hasn't had her dessert yet?"

"Neither has her assistant," Jake added with a laugh.

Robert looked up from eating. "You have to be quick in this family to get the goodies." Then he went back to finishing his pie.

Marcella took her last bite, pushed her plate away and patted her stomach. "That was the best cheesecake."

Jake's stomach rumbled.

Laughter echoed through the room.

Nancy scooted her chair back and walked toward the foyer. When she came back, she held two plates, laden with large pieces of both desserts. "Do you really think we would do that to the cook and her assistant? Although that is a dubious title for a certain person." Emma's mom looked at Jake and gave him his dessert with a smile. "Weren't you in the living room with Robert, Ben and Josh watching the game?"

"I helped yesterday with the shopping." He snatched his plate and took his seat. "That qualifies."

Ben snorted while Marcella snickered.

As Jake dug into the cheesecake, he relished

the moment. *Thank You, Lord, for showing me what it can be like. My family was never like this.*

Emma stood on the sidelines of an impromptu baseball game at the park's ball field with Jake as the pitcher while Ben played catcher and the outfielders were Craig's dad and Sandy. Emma's dad, Kim and Nancy positioned themselves at the bases. Josh, Carson and Craig each took a turn at bat.

"Josh is loving all this attention," Marcella said as she grasped Buttons's leash while Emma held Butch's and Shep's.

"All three boys are going to try out for baseball this spring. Craig played last year. Between his and Jake's help, Josh has been really improving in the past month."

"I still haven't gotten Jake to agree to teach a self-defense class at church, but I think I'm wearing him down, especially since he's started attending the Sunday service. That's what he did when he visited his grandma." Marcella turned her attention to Emma. "When he first came back here, I knew he was home, but when I went over to his house, he didn't answer the door. Finally, one day I caught him while the teen was delivering his groceries to him and barreled my way into his house. Normally I wouldn't have done that, but his grandma was my best friend. I owed her that much."

"I'm glad you did."

"He was in a bad place. At that time, he was still using crutches. I know he's dealing with more than his leg but that's none of my business. I'm just glad you're part of his life now. He needs someone to make him care again."

Emma watched Josh take a swing at the ball and miss. The next one, though, he hit and it sailed through the air. Her son ran to first base then kept going while Sandy scooped up the ball and threw it to Emma's mom. Nancy bobbled her catch, and Josh raced past her for home plate. Emma and everyone cheered him on. When Josh reached it, he pumped his arm in the air and beamed as though he were playing in the major league and had won the game for his team.

Jake limped toward Josh and gave him a high five. "That's the way to hit the ball. You're a fast learner."

"Josh needs a good man in his life," Emma said as Craig stepped up to bat.

"Jake is that, even with what he's going through," Marcella said.

"I agree." In that moment as Jake stood again on the pitcher mound, Emma knew she loved him. She hadn't wanted to fall in love, not after Sam.

But in spite of the guilt she felt for her husband's death, she had.

"Are you going to the Christmas tree lighting next weekend at the park downtown?"

"Yes, do you want to go with us?" Emma asked, remembering that Marcella drove only during the daylight hours.

She winked at Emma. "I thought you would never ask."

"You know you're always welcome."

"I didn't know if you had a date or not."

"A date? With my son?"

"No. With Jake. I know last year your son went with Craig's family so I thought this would be a great opportunity for you and Jake to go out."

"I haven't even said anything to Jake about the Christmas tree lighting. It's gotten awfully big in the past several years." She wasn't sure Jake would like it, but after how things had been going in the past couple of weeks, maybe he would.

"Ask him, and if you want to make it a two-some, just let me know. I can catch a ride with another neighbor."

Emma combed her fingers through her hair. "I will say something to him but you're going with us."

"I've already got my presents bought and wrapped. How about you?"

"Not totally. I'm not that organized." Since her

money was limited, it wouldn't take long to finish her short list. The fall had flown by and before long it would be winter—and the possibility of snow and ice. "I love Christmas, but I could do without the cold temperatures."

"Me and these old bones feel the same way."

Emma turned her attention again to the game. She scanned the baseball field and caught a glimpse of Sean, standing next to one of the dugouts watching them play. Even from a distance she could see a look of yearning on his face. The expression made her wonder what was going on with the boy lately. Josh hadn't said much to her about him. She hoped he wasn't here to make trouble or waiting for Liam and his buddies to come. Then Emma remembered all the adults surrounding her son, keeping him safe.

Josh made it to second base before he was tagged out. Jogging back toward home plate, her son passed close to Jake who said something to Josh. He swung around, saw Sean and detoured toward him. Emma tensed and began to make her way toward the pair. She couldn't see her son's face but surprise flitted across Sean's. Then the older boy nodded and disappeared behind the dugout. A few seconds later he came into view and out onto the field.

Jake stopped his windup and kept an eye on Josh and Sean as they walked to where the boys were waiting for their turn at bat. Jake headed toward the group at the same time Emma did, still holding the leashes for Butch and Shep.

As she approached, Jake said, "As long as you agree to play by the rules, we'd love to have you join us. Wouldn't we?"

Sean looked in each boy's eyes as he nodded, then said, "Yes, sir."

Emma's throat filled with emotion as the boys played for another half hour, including Sean as a friend would. Jake was worth fighting for. He was teaching her son the right way to handle problems.

The soft sounds of "What Child Is This" played in the background while Jake, seated near the eight-foot pine, handed Emma and Josh Christmas ornaments. His leg ached from pitching at the baseball game earlier then helping Ben string the lights on the artificial tree. But he didn't mind the dull pain. Today was worth it.

Emma glanced back at him. "Do you see any spots that need more decorations?"

"Are you kidding? I can't see the tree now," Jake said with a chuckle, the song ending and "Joy to the World" starting.

"It's there, under memories of my past." Emma held up a cutout from an egg carton transformed into a bell with glitter, paint and a pipe cleaner used as a hook. "Josh made this when he was three. I have a set of six."

They were all prominently displayed, Jake noted as his gaze went from one to the other. "Well spaced on the tree."

She gave him a narrow-eyed look. "Are you making fun of me?"

He held up his hands, shaking his head. "No way. I know better."

Stretched out by the chair, Shep looked up at Jake then settled back with his head resting on his front paws.

Josh giggled. "Mom never throws away an ornament until it totally falls apart or smashes. Didn't you notice Grandma, Grandpa and Uncle Ben left before she brought out the rest of the balls to put on the tree?"

Emma put her hand on her waist. "Hold it right there, you two. I warned you I had a lot. Besides, my parents and brother had to get back to Tulsa. Ben has to work tomorrow." The teasing gleam in her eyes brightened then, the sparkle competing with the lights on the tree.

Her look transfixed Jake. "About those extra boxes. I thought you told me your decorations were all out in the garage. Where did these five come from?"

"These are my special ones."

"Yeah, mostly made by me or ones from her

childhood." Josh took an ornament from Jake and loaded a branch with another ball.

"Time for a break," Marcella said, carrying in a tray with mugs of hot chocolate.

Emma took it from her and placed it on the coffee table. "We only have a couple more, then we're finished."

Jake struggled to his feet, ignoring the ache in his leg, and hung two of the last five ornaments while Josh put the others on the pine. "Done. Your timing, Marcella, is perfect." He limped toward the couch and sank onto the cushion at one end, Shep settling at his feet.

"But we still have the garland to put up." Emma opened the last box over in the corner and showed the group the shiny red strings.

"That will cover up your beautiful ornaments." Jake reached for a mug of hot chocolate, steam wafting from it.

Emma stood back from the tree and cocked her head. "You're right. Except for this one." She pulled out a length of homemade red-and-green paper rings. "Josh made this in first grade."

The child's cheeks turned a rosy tint. "Mom, do you hafta put that up?"

Emma studied the pine again then scanned the room. "No. You are right. The tree has enough, but—" she headed to the mantel and hung the paper garland along its edge "—this will be a nice addition here where it won't get lost among the ornaments."

Josh looked at Jake. "I'll never make another decoration again."

Jake laughed and handed the boy a mug, then raised his. "That's moms for you."

"Yeah, but mine goes overboard."

"I hear you, Josh." Emma finally took a seat at the other end of the couch and grabbed her drink.

Marcella leaned back in her chair across from Jake and sipped her hot chocolate. "I want to thank you, Emma, for inviting me to share your Thanksgiving dinner and meet your family. This was a treat."

"I second that." Jake lifted his mug again and tapped it against Emma's then Josh's and Marcella's. "This was a wonderful Thanksgiving, and I'm looking forward to Christmas for the first time in years." As he said those words, he realized the holidays hadn't meant much to him in the past but Emma's enthusiasm was contagious.

Emma rose and bowed. "I've done my job. I've spread my joy of the Christmas season to others. Finish your drink and then all we have to do is put away the empty boxes."

Jake groaned along with Josh and Marcella. When Emma gave each one of them a mockingly stunned look, Jake laughed. Josh joined him, followed by Marcella and Emma. Both Shep and Buttons began barking.

"You're a hard taskmaster, but since I helped make the mess, I'll help clean it up." Jake turned to Josh. "You game?"

The boy nodded.

Thirty minutes later with Shep by his side, Jake stood in the entrance to the living room, surveying his work. With all the lamps turned off, the tree dominated the area, the hundreds of lights shining. Emma came up behind him and touched his arm as she moved beside him. Her lavender scent vied with the pine aroma from a lit candle on the mantel.

She glanced toward him and took his hand. "Thanks for going along with me today."

"That was easy to do. It was fun." *I almost felt normal today.* But one good day didn't mean everything would be all right tomorrow or the following ones. He would cherish, though, the time spent today with Emma and her family.

Clear lights were strung everywhere—in the trees and on the bushes—in the downtown park across from the city hall. As Jake, with Shep by his side, strolled with Emma toward where the Christmas-tree ceremony would take place, he slipped his arm around her, their steps slowing. Marcella and Josh hurried ahead of the couple, wanting to find a good spot from which to watch. One of the town's celebrities—a pro baseball player—was throwing the switch to light the fifteen-foot pine. Josh wanted to get his autograph afterward.

Coming to a stop, Emma looked up at Jake. "This looks like a fairyland. I always love walking through here at this time of year. It's even prettier when it has snowed."

"I don't remember this ceremony being as festive and big when I was here at Christmas as a child."

"It's grown each year. Afterward, all the stores and restaurants stay open late and people linger downtown. I was hoping we could. I need to do some Christmas shopping. After the ceremony, Josh is going home with Craig to spend the night."

"How about Marcella?"

"When she heard about Josh, she told me she was grabbing a ride home with a neighbor. They were meeting at the café across the street for some dessert."

Laughter welled up in him. He clasped Emma against him. "That means we have the evening to ourselves. Interesting how those two maneuvered that."

"You think? I don't think it crossed Josh's mind, but Marcella, yes, she could have. Are we still on for decorating a tree at your house tomorrow?"

"Just because you put yours up Thanksgiving night, doesn't mean I have to have one."

"Yes, it does. When I look at mine, I think of all the past Christmases. The ornaments from friends and family bring back fond memories, but they also make me realize why we celebrate Christmas. With Christ's birth, the world changed forever. He gives me hope. Sometimes I need that reminder."

He did more than ever. Somewhere along the way Jake had lost hope. God and Emma were teaching him how to find it again. "Put that way, how can I refuse?"

"You can't. Besides, all those ornaments your grandma kept will be put to good use."

He brushed his hand through her hair, loving the feel of it sliding through his fingers. "Thanks for helping me to get them down from the attic. It's still hard for me to climb all those steps to the third floor, and with the amount she had I would have had to do it several times."

She smiled, her eyes sparkling like the lights all around them. "Anytime."

As people headed for the ceremony, they skirted around Jake and Emma on the path. He pulled her off the trail to allow everyone to pass and for a little privacy. He wasn't in any hurry to be with a crowd.

"You're beautiful, Emma, inside and out."

"You ain't too bad to look at yourself! But I

can't thank you enough for what you've done to help Josh. Since Thanksgiving and the baseball game, Josh told me Sean has talked to him at school as a friend. Sean doesn't seem to be involved with Liam much anymore."

"Liam has a lot of anger inside him. I hope he gets the help he needs."

"See what I mean. You're a fine man."

He smiled, slowly lowering his head toward hers. The few kisses they'd shared only left him wanting more, and with his better outlook lately, maybe they had a chance for being more than just friends.

"I know we need to get to the ceremony before Josh comes looking for us, but I can't resist..." He whispered the words over her parted lips and bridged the gap.

Pop! Pop! Pop!

The sound of gunfire sent him in motion. He was suddenly back in the mountain village. He dived for the ground and cover, taking Emma with him, shielding her as best as he could.

Chapter Thirteen

As Emma lay plastered against the cold ground, Jake's body over hers, she felt him shaking, his heartbeat hammering against his chest.

The popping sound of the firecrackers resonated through the chilly air, the noise similar to rapid gunfire. She wiggled out from under a paralyzed Jake, frozen in probably a flashback, sweat drenching his face.

As she freed herself, she noticed a crowd forming around them, Josh's eyes huge, fear on his face. "Please get back," she said to the people, then turned toward Jake, Shep nudging him and barking.

In her calmest voice, Emma said, "Jake. Jake. You're in Cimarron City at the park. Those were firecrackers going off. Probably some kids."

He stared at her, but she didn't think he was really seeing her. Her concern mounted, especially with the crowd still pressing close.

She stood, gesturing with her hands to move back.

Someone said, "Should I call 911?"

"No, that's not necessary." That was the last thing Jake would want.

An older man plowed through the people. "I'm a doctor. Can I help? Is he having a seizure?"

"No, a panic attack," Emma said as quietly as she could but several people heard her, including her son. Josh's face went pale.

When the onlookers began to disperse, Josh stepped back but didn't leave.

Emma went back to Jake, not touching him but near if he needed her. "Let's breathe deeply on my count. Inhale one, two. Exhale one, two." She continued until she reached the count of four.

Jake's stiff body began to relax. His awareness of his surroundings came back, and he scanned the area. His gaze latched on to Josh, then Marcella, who came up behind him.

"Shep's here to help," Emma said to pull his attention from Josh. "Everything's all right."

"What was that sound?" Jake finally asked.

"Firecrackers." When he seemed calm, no longer shaking or sweating, she asked, "Do you want to go to the ceremony?"

His eyes widened. "No. Home."

"Fine. Let me tell Josh and Marcella." As she

approached them, Jake struggled to his feet, still stroking the top of Shep's head.

"What happened, Mom? What's a panic attack?"

Emma glanced at Jake to make sure he hadn't heard her son. "He thought the firecrackers were a gun going off."

"He's like Uncle Ben?"

"Yes, hon. Marcella, will you make sure Josh connects with Craig and his parents?"

"I will. Come on, Josh. We don't want to miss the ceremony and your chance to get an autograph."

The boy peered back as he walked away, his brow knitted, uncertainty making him hesitate.

"See you tomorrow at church, hon."

"He knows about me?" His voice bleak, Jake stood right behind her.

"Yes. Let's go."

"I want you to drop me off and then you can come back here. I know you wanted to do some shopping. I don't want this to stop you."

She didn't answer. She decided to give him some time and distance from the incident. But she wasn't dropping him off and leaving him alone. She loved him and wanted to be near if he needed help.

At his house, a familiar environment where firecrackers wouldn't send him into a panic, thinking he was back in Afghanistan being shot at, Jake finally released the last bit of tension gripping him. He turned in the foyer and spread his arms wide. "See. I'm fine. You can leave now."

"No, I'd rather stay with you."

"But I don't want you to."

Hurt darkened Emma's blue eyes, and her shoulders sagged slightly. "Because of what happened at the park? I've seen panic attacks. What happened to you is nothing new. You had one. It's over. Move on."

Her tough, matter-of-fact words hit him as though she'd slapped him. "I tackled you to the ground. Aren't you just a little embarrassed?"

"If that had been a real gun going off, you could have saved my life. You reacted to a noise that was similar. You have been trained to react quickly. Firecrackers aren't supposed to go off in the city limits so it was an unexpected sound."

"Quit trying to rationalize something that isn't rational."

"Don't start feeling sorry for yourself. You're improving, but that won't happen overnight. Ben still has some problems. Acknowledge the panic attacks, deal with them then let them go. Don't let them rule your life."

"You don't know what you're talking about. You haven't dealt with panic attacks."

"No, but I lived with a husband who had epilepsy for most of our marriage. His seizures would happen unexpectedly, and we had to deal with them. We knew what to do, what not to do…" Her voice disappeared as she gulped.

There was that look she got when talking about her husband. Regrets she'd married a person with epilepsy—deeply flawed the way he was? A seizure led to his death. "What aren't you telling me? Every time we start to talk about your husband, you put a distance between us. I've told you about my relationship with my father, about my panic attacks."

She averted her gaze, staring into the living room. Her teeth bit into her lower lip. Her hands balled. "My husband died because of me."

He'd expected her to say a lot of things but not that. "He fell off a ladder. How are you responsible?"

When she peered at him, sadness dulled her eyes. "Josh and I were talking about decorating the outside of the house with lights the way we'd decorated the inside. My husband overheard, and before I told him I was hiring the teenage boy next door to put them up, he was doing it. He shouldn't have been up that high, especially without someone there and with concrete below him."

"And you blame yourself?"

"Yes. I knew that Sam thought he could do everything like a normal person—that he didn't have to keep in mind his seizure disorder. He hated that I had to drive him everywhere. I should never have said anything to Josh with my husband in the house."

"Your husband is responsible for his own actions. He knew he shouldn't get up on a ladder like that. You're not at fault. It was an accident."

"I should have been able to protect him. He had epilepsy. I needed to be there for him."

"Smothering him?"

"I—I didn't think so. I always looked at it as though we were in it together." She closed the space between them. "I can't turn my back on someone I care about. Someone I love." She swallowed hard. "Like you."

He wanted to pretend he hadn't heard what she'd said, but he couldn't. He could never ask her to tie herself to a man who was damaged and needed fixing. What if he never got better? He thought he was, and then he'd had a full-blown attack in public—for Josh to see. "You're a caregiver. That isn't love. Go back to the ceremony. Enjoy yourself."

"I don't want to leave. We need to deal with this together."

"Why? So you can manage my life? I don't want that. I want to be cured. I want to be normal."

"What's normal for one isn't what is for another."

"I should have known those were firecrackers. I've heard them before. I used to set them off as a kid. I couldn't stop the panic attack. Please leave." He strode to the door and opened it. "Thanks for bringing me home." He stared into space, avoiding meeting her eyes. He might give in and try to hold on to her when it wasn't fair to Emma to saddle her with another man like her husband—broken.

Surrounded by all her Christmas decorations with the pine tree full of ornaments in front of the picture window in the living room—the one Jake had helped her put up—Emma paced while Abbey sat on the couch and watched her. "I don't know what to do. Jake isn't answering the door or his phone. Last Sunday Josh and I left the Christmas tree we were going to decorate together on his porch. I know he's there because the tree's gone. It's been four days since what happened Saturday night at the lighting of the Christmas tree ceremony. He's gone back to being a hermit."

"He did come to Monday night's session. We don't have our private one until tomorrow. I could go by today and see if he'll talk to me."

"Please try to get him to talk about Saturday night. He told me he wanted to be normal. He wouldn't believe me when I said normalcy is relative. I think he feels like he's beaten, may always be that way."

"I'll try my best. The good news is he came on Monday night so he hasn't given up. He's just frustrated."

Stopping her pacing, Emma intertwined her fingers, clasping them together until her knuckles whitened. "I told him I loved him Saturday. He said what I'm feeling isn't love." She connected visually with Abbey. "I love him. His having PTSD doesn't change how I feel. Sam's having epilepsy didn't change how I felt about him."

"Give him time to get a grasp on what he's dealing with. He's gone through a lot in the past eight months."

"I know. I didn't set out to fall in love, and I didn't mean to say it to him, especially right after a panic attack."

"I'm working with him on some techniques, but they will take time to become automatic and feel natural to him. What he said just came out."

Emma's eyes blurred with unshed tears. She'd cried for the past few nights, wishing they hadn't gone to the ceremony. But that panic attack in such a public place could have happened at another time. Not going wouldn't have necessarily changed the end result. "I told him about feeling guilty concerning Sam's death." Since she hadn't told anyone but Jake, she explained to Abbey.

"Did he tell you it wasn't your fault?"

Emma nodded.

"He's right. People are responsible for their own actions. You can't control everything. When Sam died, you felt your life do an about-face. Suddenly, you were going in a different direction—a single mom with a debt to pay off. Don't put more burdens on yourself by feeling guilty. God has a wonderful way of forgiving anyone who repents and asks for forgiveness. If you need to, ask him to forgive you and then let it go. Give control over to the Lord. He'll take you on a wild and exciting ride." Abbey stood, rolling her shoulders.

Emma closed the space between them and hugged her. "Thanks. I should have told you when Sam died how I was feeling, but I was afraid of what you would think of me."

"The only thing you should care about is what God thinks of you. When you have Him in your corner, everything else falls into place."

Emma thought about what Abbey had said about guilt and control. She needed to let both of them go. Whether or not Jake wanted to continue one day in a relationship, she needed to say goodbye to the past.

Jake stared at the Christmas tree Emma and Josh had delivered on Sunday, bare of any decorations. A box of four ornaments—homemade by Emma and Josh—sat next to the live pine, its scent permeating the room. They still were in the carton. He couldn't put them or the boxes of ornaments that were his grandma's on the branches.

When the doorbell rang, he considered ignoring whoever was there, but he couldn't keep doing that. Marcella had left him some cinnamon rolls yesterday, and the worried look on her face had almost made him answer the door.

When the chimes filled the air again, he rose and plodded toward the foyer. When he saw Abbey, he hesitated then realized this couldn't keep going on. He might not be able to have the type of relationship with Emma he wanted, but he had to get on with his life. Abbey could help him.

He let her in. "Our next session isn't until tomorrow."

"Yes, but I thought we could talk today, too. Except for the Monday night group, have you left this house since Saturday night?"

"No, but that was only four days ago. Not that unusual for me."

"I would agree if we were talking about a month ago. Let's talk." Abbey marched into his living room and took a seat in a chair. "I have some material for you. I would like you to read it today, and then we'll discuss it tomorrow. It's a method to help you overcome your panic attacks beyond what you're doing. It's reprogramming how you think about the attacks when they begin."

He sank down on the couch across from her, his gaze momentarily lingering on the Christmas tree behind Abbey.

"You need to accept this will take time and that's okay. You've come a long way in the past two months, and you'll go further, but not overnight."

"In other words, I shouldn't become a recluse because of what happened Saturday night in front of a crowd."

"Exactly."

"Have you seen Emma?" He didn't want to ask but couldn't stop himself.

"I saw her this morning before she left for work, and she's worried about you. You canceled the self-defense class for Tuesday. You aren't answering her calls or the door. She gets it—you don't want to talk to her. But you didn't answer for Marcella or Sandy when they came by, either."

"I made a fool of myself in front of so many people. In front of Josh."

"He knows you have PTSD and understands. His uncle does, and he loves Ben. Emma talked to Josh on Sunday. To him it doesn't mean anything. You are his hero."

"I'm no one's hero."

"Because you survived when some of your men didn't?"

He nodded.

"God has special plans for you, and you can't argue with the Lord. So what are you going to do about it?"

He stared at the material she'd placed on the coffee table. "I'll start by reading this, then I'll meet with you tomorrow."

Abbey pushed to her feet. "Then I'll leave you to get started."

After she was gone, he began reading what she had brought him. When he finished, he looked up and caught sight of the Christmas tree. He remembered what Emma said about seeing hers and feeling hope. He rose and went to the box with the four ornaments in it. He took each one out and put it on the pine.

The next day Jake faced the four boys in his workout room with Sandy off to the side. She'd brought them, and he'd asked her to stay for a few minutes. He scanned the face of each one, and all he saw in their expressions was respect—nothing different from before. His chest tightened.

He cleared his throat. "I'm sorry I canceled Tuesday afternoon, but after what happened Saturday, I had some thinking to do. I have panic attacks occasionally. In the case of Saturday night the sound of firecrackers going off caused me to react as though I was under fire. I'm working to deal with my panic attacks, but it'll take time. I'll understand if you don't want to continue with the self-defense classes."

Josh's face screwed up in a puzzled look. "What does that have to do with our class?"

"Yeah, I want to keep learning," Craig said with the other guys nodding.

Sandy moved between the children and Jake. "We have faith in you. These boys look forward to these classes. You have made them feel like they can handle anything. They feel better about themselves, not to mention you took care of the bullying."

The constriction in his chest eased as he swept his gaze from one child to the next. *Sandy has it wrong. These guys have made me feel better about myself.* "Then let's get going. We have a lot to do today. First, let's stretch."

An hour later Jake realized how important these sessions with the four had been for him, too. They had looked to him for guidance and help, and he'd been able to give it to them. Maybe he would be able to deal with his own problems.

When Emma showed up to take the boys home, he didn't know what to say to her. She deserved more than he could give her. He didn't know how long it would take for him to overcome his PTSD.

Emma said, "Josh, you and the guys go on out to the car. I'll be there in a minute."

Then Emma turned to Jake with a neutral expression. Slowly, hurt invaded her eyes. "I wanted to thank you for doing this for them. Josh was so disappointed not to be able to come on Tuesday, but he understood you needed time and so did I." Her voice became husky. "My feelings are the same whether you have a panic attack or not. That doesn't define you as a person in my mind." She waited a moment for him to say something and, when he didn't, she swung around and left.

He knew he loved her as he watched her walk away, but no words came to mind to say to her. He couldn't come to her the way he was now.

In the pitch dark Jake woke up to the sound of ice pelting his bedroom window. He tried his lamp on the nightstand but nothing happened. His battery-operated clock read six o'clock. The chill in the air indicated the electricity had been off for hours.

The predicted ice storm must have moved in last night. He needed to get up and check outside. If it didn't look as if the electricity was coming on anytime soon, he would use the generator he'd bought for an emergency like this. But the warmth under his covers enticed him to stay in bed until it was light enough to see rather than make his way to the kitchen in the dark to get his flashlight.

The continual bombarding of the ice against his house set off alarm bells in his mind. He hadn't been in an ice storm in years, but it could leave a town crippled if it lasted long. Did Emma have a generator to warm at least part of her house? The temperature high for the next few days was only supposed to be in the mid-twenties. Maybe in the morning he'd try calling her if the phones still worked and find out if she was all right. He'd feel better—

The blare of his phone startled him. His heartbeat accelerated as he fumbled for it on the bedside table. "Hello."

"Jake, a tree fell on our house. Mom's trapped in her bedroom." Tears laced Josh's urgent words.

"I'll be right there, Josh. Is she hurt?"

"She says no but she can't get out and the ice is falling on her. I called 911, but they can't get here for a while."

Throwing back the covers, Jake swung his legs over the side of the bed, then rose. "Don't go in there. Tell her I'm coming."

"Hurry. I'm scared."

In the dark Jake searched for the jeans and sweatshirt he'd tossed toward the chair last night. When he found them, he dressed quickly, telling himself over and over Emma and Josh were okay.

He would get them and bring them back here. But his heart pounded against his rib cage, and his chest felt tight.

Feeling his way to the kitchen, he went through his mental routine to keep him focused on getting to Emma's without having a panic attack. After he retrieved the large flashlight, he looked for a saw in his toolbox, then started for the front door.

The sky a dark gray, Jake paused on his porch to figure the best way to go while he swept his flashlight in a wide arc over the terrain. Ice coated everything at least an inch thick, glittering when his light hit it. Although the landscape was beautiful to behold, to be out in it was dangerous. Fortunately, snow was beginning to fall and would allow him to walk better.

Bundled up, Jake descended the steps, gripping the railing, then headed out into the mixture of falling snow and ice. *Lord, please keep Emma and Josh safe. Help me to get there before any harm is done.*

The silence was eerie until a loud noise like the crack of a rifle reverberated in the air. Adrenaline pumped through him. Instead of tensing, he breathed from the diaphragm, slow, deep inhalations. He began to relax, even when another cracking noise—louder, nearer—echoed through the quiet. A limb on Marcella's oak in the front snapped and crashed to the ground. When Emma and Josh were safe back at his house, he would check on his neighbor.

As Jake crept toward the middle of the street where there were no overhead branches to break off and fall on him, he kept taking in and releasing those deep breaths while acknowledging he was having a panic attack. "I'm okay. This gives me a chance to prove to myself I can cope. There's nothing to be afraid of. The sounds aren't gunfire but limbs breaking off trees."

He headed toward Emma's as fast as he could, praying the whole way. With each step he took he felt more capable of handling his panic attack, even though he continued to hear branches snapping off nearby as well as in the distance. The rapid beat of his heart slowed. The trembling faded.

In the distance he saw a light flash in the sky and a loud boom resonated through the air. *Just a transformer going. That's all. I'm okay.*

By the time he reached Emma's block, all signs of a panic attack were gone, although the loud noises still sounded in the biting, cold wind. When he'd had an attack before, he'd always gotten upset, making it worse. Abbey had been working with him to accept what was happening to him, and then move on.

And he had. He smiled. *Thank You, Lord.*

Then he spied Emma's house two down from

the corner. A large elm tree had split and fallen on the right side of her place—where her bedroom was. He tried increasing his pace, but he slipped and went down on the knee of his good leg. Catching himself by clutching a mailbox, he used it to pull himself up then slowed his steps. *With the Lord and patience, I'll make it.*

Dressed in a heavy coat, sweats and gloves, Josh opened the door before Jake made it halfway up the sidewalk to the porch. Worry lined the boy's face.

When he started to come outside, Jake said, "Don't. Close the door. I'll be there in a minute," then he proceeded at his slow pace.

When he made it inside Emma's house, he heard the whistle of the wind coming from the hallway to the right. "How's your mom?"

"She says okay, but I can hear her teeth chattering."

Jake covered the distance to the hallway and started down it, noticing the bedroom door was closed.

"Mom made me shut it to keep as much heat in the house as possible."

"Good thinking." Jake swung the door open, saying, "Stay here. If I need you, I'll call you," then he closed himself in the room with Emma, assessing the situation.

"I'm sorry you had to get out in this. I asked

Josh to call 911. He did, but they won't be here for a while since I'm not hurt. I told him I could wait. Instead, he called you."

"As I told him a few seconds ago, good thinking."

Jake examined the split half of the elm, a large branch falling across Emma's bed, several smaller limbs trapping her. A coverlet blanketed her but so did a layer of ice and now snow. Her face pale, she shivered, her lips turning blue.

Jake set down his flashlight so it shone on what he needed to cut. "Do you have something plastic I can cover you with? It'll keep the snow and ice off while I saw you out of there."

"A raincoat…oh, and I have a plastic tablecloth. It's bigger than the raincoat. It's in the cabinet in the utility room."

Jake climbed over the branches between him and the one he needed to remove. "Josh." When the boy came into the room, Jake said, "I need you to fetch a plastic tablecloth." After Jake told him where it was, Josh left, and Jake started sawing the biggest limb.

When Josh returned, he wiggled through the limbs and handed Jake the tablecloth. "I wanna stay and help."

Emma said, "I want you to stay out—"

Jake interrupted, "Sure. I need you to hold the

flashlight." As the child grabbed it, Jake whispered to Emma, "He needs to know you're okay."

Emma attempted a smile that stayed a few seconds. "I know but it's so cold."

"I'm fine, Mom."

With snow swirling on the wind coming through the hole, Jake spread the plastic over Emma to protect her then returned to sawing. He put all his strength into it, and minutes later he caught the first branch before it fell on Emma. Adrenaline still surging through him, he heaved it over to the side and let it go, then began on the second limb.

Soon he severed that branch from the split trunk and tossed it to the right. "Do you think you can crawl out now?" he asked, but Emma, dressed in sweats, was already wiggling out from under the coverlet.

Jake clasped her arm and tugged her the rest of the way loose, then assisted her over the limbs. When he got a good hold of her, he swung her up into his arms and followed Josh from the room. The boy slammed the door, cutting off the wind, but the temperature was probably thirty-five in the hallway.

Clasping Emma against him, Jake strode toward the living room. "Josh, get some blankets for your mom." Jake placed her on the couch, then covered her with what Josh brought.

With Emma wrapped in two blankets, Jake

rubbed his hands up and down her arms to get the blood circulating. "I'm warming you up, then we're going to my house."

"But we can't—"

"Shh. No arguments. I have a big generator, and the last I knew no holes in my roof. You promised to help me decorate my Christmas tree. I'm here to remind you of that."

She stared at him then burst out laughing. Jake and Josh looked at each other, then broke out into smiles.

"Josh, call 911 back and let them know I've been rescued."

The child hurried from the room.

Emma's gaze snared Jake's. "Thank you, Jake. I don't know what I would have done."

"My pleasure. And when you two are settled at my house, we need to talk." His arms enveloped her, and he pulled her against him. If she had been lying on the bed a few inches to her left, she could have been crushed beneath the tree. *Thank You, Lord.*

Glancing at her Christmas tree laden with ornaments in front of the window, he had real peace for the first time in a long while. Christmas was only a few days away. If the electricity wasn't restored, Emma and Josh would be spending it with him. That thought brightened his spirits even more. In that moment, he realized he was ready to move on—to a life with or without panic attacks.

Later that evening, Emma stood back from Jake's smaller live Christmas tree and studied the display she, Josh, Jake and Marcella had worked on for the past hour. The sound of Christmas music filled the room from a battery-powered radio.

After Emma had been rescued from her house, Jake had made his way to Marcella's and brought her over because she had no generator. Then they had been busy consolidating what they would need into a couple of rooms on the first floor that would be heated with the generator and fireplace.

Jake had wanted to talk with Emma, but they'd been busy. Now that she had stopped and sat next to Marcella on his couch, exhaustion began to weave its way through her. From the tired lines on Marcella's face, Jake could tell she was also bone-weary.

"Josh, you said you wanted to put the star on top of the tree." Jake presented him with a beautiful glittered and sequined ornament.

Josh grinned, climbed up on the step stool and placed the last decoration on the pine. "Perfect."

First Shep barked then Buttons, as though to give their approval.

"I agree. Now to turn on the lights." Jake plugged them in.

The soft glow from the tree along with the blaze in the fireplace illuminated the room.

"I know we're two weeks late decorating your tree, but I think we did good." Emma leaned forward to gather up the mugs they had hot apple cider in. "Time to clean up the mess we made."

Jake looked at Josh. "Is your mom always like this?"

"Yep."

"I've still got to clean up from dinner, so the least you all could do is put the empty ornament boxes away."

"I'm not climbing those stairs again today. We'll store them in my bedroom. Wanna help me, Josh?"

The boy started picking up some to carry down the hallway.

"I'll help you, Emma." Marcella began to rise from the couch.

"No, you stay in here and relax. It's been a long day," Emma said then hurried away before Marcella protested.

The furnace, refrigerator, stove, hot water heater and a few lights were running on Jake's generator stored in the garage. With some conservation of electrical usage, the generator kept the house comfortable for them. While listening to the radio, Emma washed the dishes in hot water, a luxury she wouldn't take for granted again. "Silent Night" came on the station, and Emma began singing the song.

When she finished, applause sounded behind her. She whirled around to find Jake standing in the entrance, lounging against the doorjamb. Her pulse rate kicked up a notch.

"The news on the radio doesn't sound promising for getting our electricity anytime soon," Emma said, drying her hands, her throat tight with emotion. Peace and joy filled her.

His gaze roped hers, and he moved toward her. "Towns all around us are affected. They're going to have to bring people in from other areas to help."

"I've never heard ice breaking limbs like that— almost nonstop as we walked here."

"It sounded like a war zone."

She hadn't wanted to use that analogy, but he was right. "You were okay."

"I was—even when I had an attack on the way over to your house. I've been working on changing my attitude about my panic attacks. I'm not going to let them control my life anymore."

She threw her arms around his neck and drew him against her. "Mmm. You're warm. I never thought I would thaw out this morning, but your house became toasty in a few hours. I know I've thanked you for—"

He claimed her mouth in a deep kiss she felt down to the tips of her toes. "I love you."

He said the words she'd dreamed he would but she didn't want to misread what he meant. "I love you, too, but you know that. I want more from you. A life together as a family." Emma cuddled closer.

Leaning back slightly, he looked deep into her eyes with a half smile on his face. "It won't always be easy, but would you be interested in a guy with a slight problem?"

"Who doesn't have a problem?" Her embrace tightened. She never wanted to let go. "What changed your mind?"

"You, Josh and Abbey. She has been working double-time to get me to a place where I don't let the panic attacks overwhelm me before I have a chance to deal with them. I'm learning to ride them out and lessen their effects. It won't be perfect, but far better than it was. Today demonstrated that to me. A month ago that cracking noise would have sent me into a full-blown attack, like the one I had at the Christmas-tree lighting ceremony. The crack-pop sounds so close to gunfire in a battle."

"I love you, Jake. I want it all. Marriage. A family. Josh looks up to you, even after witnessing that attack. That didn't change his mind and it certainly didn't mine." She watched for any negative reaction from him.

Instead, an expression full of happiness graced his face. "I was embarrassed and scared. I reacted by pushing everyone away. As a soldier I've learned not to show my weaknesses, but I have them."

"Like everyone else. God made us with strengths and weaknesses and loves us, anyway."

"I know that now. It took some soul searching and some conversations with Him to finally figure that out."

She slid her hands to his face, framing it. "If I ever gave you the idea that Sam's seizures made me regret marrying him, then I'm here to correct that impression. When I married him, it was for better or worse, and in every marriage you have both."

"Have you forgiven yourself for his accident?" Jake closed the inches separating them and feathered his mouth across hers.

"Yes, both you and Abbey helped me to see it wasn't my fault."

"I'm looking forward to the future. I want to help others the way you and Abbey do. Once I earn my doctorate, I'm thinking of working with veterans, especially ones with PTSD. Who better than someone who's dealt with it?"

"Perfect." Emma slanted her head to the side and kissed him with all the love she felt in her heart.

Epilogue

One year later on Christmas Eve...

Emma snuggled closer to her husband of three months on the couch in front of the fireplace, adorned with a combination of her and his decorations. "I loved the service at church this evening, especially since we missed last year's because of the ice storm."

Jake laughed. "We did have a white Christmas last year. This one is going to be a balmy fifty-eight if the weatherman is right."

Emma's glance strayed to the Christmas tree, so loaded down with the ornaments, she worried it would collapse under the weight. "I'm surprised Josh could get to sleep. Good idea about you two going to the park earlier and jogging."

"That's because I wanted you all to myself to-night. Tomorrow your parents, Ben, my dad and stepmother will be here for dinner and the opening of the presents."

"Your father and his wife should have stayed here."

Jake kissed first one corner of her mouth then the other. "We're newlyweds, and they wanted us to have some privacy."

"With a twelve-year-old here. Some privacy."

"As a family." His mouth touched hers.

When he leaned back, Emma grinned. "I thought last Christmas was perfect even with the ice storm, but this one is going to beat it hands down."

"I want to give you my gift now."

"I get to go first. I've been dying to ever since I got it this week." Emma hopped up and went to the Christmas tree set before the front window, its lights blazing, and dug around the packages under it until she pulled the wrapped gift out from the back. "I hid it so a certain person who will remain nameless didn't try to discover what it is." She laid a gold-foiled square box in his lap.

He tore into it and slowly lifted up baby booties, staring at them for a long moment.

"Just in case you haven't figured it out, I'm pregnant. Eight weeks."

An awed expression descended over his features. "I don't think I'll ever get a better gift than this for Christmas."

"So you like it?"

"Like, no. Love, yes." He planted a kiss on her mouth, all his love poured into it. "My gift pales in comparison to yours."

"I'll cherish anything you give me."

Jake pulled out the drawer of the end table next to him and gave her a small, wrapped present in red-and-green paper.

She had it open in two seconds. Her gaze glued to the beautiful gold heart locket, she held it up, dangling from her fingers. "Perfect."

He took it and showed her the two pictures inside—one of him and the other of Josh.

She twisted around and lifted her hair off her neck. "Please put it on."

After he did, he took her hand and kissed it. She'd captured the heart of a hero.

* * * * *

Dear Reader,

Her Holiday Hero is the second book in the Caring Canines series. I've had many dogs in my life, and more recently three cats. They have brought much joy and laughter to me and my family. They're so accepting and give us unconditional love. When it's been a stressful day, I like to hold my cat, hear him purring. How has having a pet made a difference in your life? Drop me a line and let me know.

I also wanted to show how a service dog trained to help someone suffering from post traumatic stress disorder can be so valuable. Remember, PTSD doesn't happen just to soldiers, but to anyone who has had a traumatic experience. And these wonderful dogs help people get back to a semblance of a normal life.

I love hearing from readers. You can contact me at margaretdaley@gmail.com or at 1316 S. Peoria Ave., Tulsa, OK 74120. You can also learn more about my books at www.margaretdaley.com. I have a quarterly newsletter that you can sign up for on my website.

Best wishes,

Margaret Daley

Questions for Discussion

1. Jake has post traumatic stress disorder (PTSD). Do you know anyone who has PTSD? What are some things you can do to help someone with this disorder?

2. For months, Jake denied that he had PTSD. Have you ever denied something was wrong with you? What did you end up doing about it?

3. Emma believes in the power of animals to help people in pain. Do you have a pet? Has your pet ever sensed you were hurting and tried to comfort you?

4. Jake had nightmares about his war experiences. Have you ever suffered from nightmares? How did you get the rest and comfort you needed?

5. Emma was having trouble with her son. He kept quiet about being bullied at school. Did your child ever not tell you about something that was going on in his/her life? What did you do about it?

6. Bullying is a big issue today. It often starts in school and then carries over into the adult

world. What are some things schools can do to stop it?

7. Jake taught Josh not only how to defend himself, but also how to evade a bully. What would you tell a child about someone bullying him?

8. Emma thought she was responsible for her husband's death because she wanted Christmas lights hung up on the house. She had a hard time forgiving herself and moving on. Has that ever happened to you? What did you do?

9. Jake received a medal for valor for his actions during the ambush that killed many of his comrades. He didn't feel like a hero and didn't think he should get the medal. What is a hero? What qualities make a hero?

10. Jake had a strained relationship with his father. He didn't feel he had lived up to what his father wanted for him. Have you felt as if you've let someone down? How did you deal with that?

LARGER-PRINT BOOKS!

GET 2 FREE
LARGER-PRINT NOVELS
PLUS 2 FREE
MYSTERY GIFTS

Love Inspired®

Larger-print novels are now available...

YES! Please send me 2 FREE LARGER-PRINT Love Inspired® novels and my 2 FREE mystery gifts (gifts are worth about $10). After receiving them, if I don't wish to receive any more books, I can return the shipping statement marked "cancel." If I don't cancel, I will receive 6 brand-new novels every month and be billed just $5.24 per book in the U.S. or $5.74 per book in Canada. That's a savings of at least 23% off the cover price. It's quite a bargain! Shipping and handling is just 50¢ per book in the U.S. and 75¢ per book in Canada.* I understand that accepting the 2 free books and gifts places me under no obligation to buy anything. I can always return a shipment and cancel at any time. Even if I never buy another book, the two free books and gifts are mine to keep forever.

122/322 IDN F49Y

Name _____ (PLEASE PRINT)

Address _____ Apt. #

City _____ State/Prov. _____ Zip/Postal Code

Signature (if under 18, a parent or guardian must sign)

Mail to the Harlequin® Reader Service:
IN U.S.A.: P.O. Box 1867, Buffalo, NY 14240-1867
IN CANADA: P.O. Box 609, Fort Erie, Ontario L2A 5X3

**Are you a current subscriber to Love Inspired books
and want to receive the larger-print edition?
Call 1-800-873-8635 or visit www.ReaderService.com.**

* Terms and prices subject to change without notice. Prices do not include applicable taxes. Sales tax applicable in N.Y. Canadian residents will be charged applicable taxes. Offer not valid in Quebec. This offer is limited to one order per household. Not valid for current subscribers to Love Inspired Larger-Print books. All orders subject to credit approval. Credit or debit balances in a customer's account(s) may be offset by any other outstanding balance owed by or to the customer. Please allow 4 to 6 weeks for delivery. Offer available while quantities last.

Your Privacy—The Harlequin® Reader Service is committed to protecting your privacy. Our Privacy Policy is available online at www.ReaderService.com or upon request from the Harlequin Reader Service.

We make a portion of our mailing list available to reputable third parties that offer products we believe may interest you. If you prefer that we not exchange your name with third parties, or if you wish to clarify or modify your communication preferences, please visit us at www.ReaderService.com/consumerschoice or write to us at Harlequin Reader Service Preference Service, P.O. Box 9062, Buffalo, NY 14269. Include your complete name and address.

LILPDIR13R

LARGER-PRINT BOOKS!

**GET 2 FREE
LARGER-PRINT NOVELS
PLUS 2 FREE
MYSTERY GIFTS**

Love Inspired®
SUSPENSE
RIVETING INSPIRATIONAL ROMANCE

Larger-print novels are now available...

ReaderService.com

Manage your account online!

- Review your order history
- Manage your payments
- Update your address

*We've designed
the Harlequin® Reader Service
website just for you.*

Enjoy all the features!

- Reader excerpts from any series
- Respond to mailings and
  special monthly offers
- Discover new series available to you
- Browse the Bonus Bucks catalog
- Share your feedback

Visit us at:
ReaderService.com

RS13